Choir Boy

by Mike Morey

also by Mike Morey:

Uncle Dirty
Anonymous
The Last Templeton

Morey, Mike
Choir Boy: a novel / Mike Morey
ISBN 978-0-359-01262-5

Cover design: Augusta DeRooter

for Jeannette

Chapter 1

I am a good boy. Ask anyone. I am the envy of mothers everywhere. Only my own flesh-and-blood might assert that I occasionally spend a little extra time in the shower, a well earned luxury that has admittedly been known to cause a morningtime bottleneck in the upstairs hallway. As the members of my family jostle for position outside the door of the only bathroom in our house, they negotiate, bicker, elbow each other's ribs until one of them pulls rank —usually my father, a bulwark of punctuality. I invariably fail to hear their raucous quarrelling over the rush of the shower nozzle.

"Look how squeaky clean I am," I shout above their petty gripes, as I emerge from my vaporous cocoon. "Those of you with zits can take an important lesson from Dado. Make way. I must dress for school."

While my cowed siblings digest my words and rub their spotty chins, my father vanishes into the mist, slams the bathroom door. For the most part, seniority rules in our house.

I am the eldest of six boys, an otherwise noisy and unsanitary line-up that runs the evolutionary gamut, like the science-class poster illustrating the chain from monkey to man, where I am represented, naturally, furthest to the right, as a fully-developed male specimen, standing erect, handsome, perceptibly intelligent. Those extra twenty minutes under the hot shower nozzle make all the difference, I say. Furthest left, my youngest brother Peck is hunched over in a chimp-like fashion, fascinated still by all things to be found on the ground, each of which must be methodically tasted before a positive identification can be made. He is nine, and has no spots on his chin. In two years, the outbreak of his acne will herald, I have no doubt, the onset of the most devastating pox yet to afflict my family. The pox will debilitate him, scar his psyche, leave him, in later years, with crippling emotional baggage, even after the spots have faded. Because of his dismal future, Peck is the only one in the monkey chain I acknowledge. I feel sorry for him, already. He will have trouble with girls.

Now that my spot-free skin is clean and pink, I will dress for my role as the clean-cut son, the model student. This important daily ritual never fails to focus my mind on what will undoubtedly be my brilliant future.

I have already decided that I will become an actor. If I have learned anything from my research into the lives of the twentieth century's rich and powerful men, it is that all the important decisions must be made early, before the vagaries of life intervene. Without a carefully laid out plan, I might otherwise be on track to become a pharmacist, or a sales rep for some third-rate luggage manufacturer. Fate has bigger plans for me. The stage is, as it were, set.

And once I have achieved this lofty goal, I will repel any and all attempts to compel me to sell out to Hollywood, the way Richard Burton did. The live stage will be the platform from which my star will glitter. My words will fill up the grey lives of the plebeian masses, will thwart suicides, will breech the delicate walls of young hearts, will spur a few to great deeds…

Provided, of course, that I survive this most trying and perilous stage in life: adolescence.

Not that I anticipate an untimely death. Like all teenagers, I believe I am immortal, or at least largely impervious to the tragedies that make sensational headlines in the daily papers. Still, I see the current age as one full of random and unforeseeable danger. There are too many cars, and too many bombs, and a surfeit of lunatics roaming the streets, even in my own neighbourhood. There was a time when the lunatics were taken away and locked up. I have investigated this subject in books and periodicals; I watch the television news; the evidence is there. The New Economics has forced impotent wardens to throw open the gates to the Booby Hatch, and now the fruitcakes roam the city like zombies, mumbling inanities, ticking time-bombs. And although the unlikely prospect of having my skull split open by some nut carries a certain melodramatic flair, I am statistically at greater risk of dying from meningitis or an aneurysm. So, while the left side of my brain is adamant in its refusal to believe that anything bad could ever happen to me, the right side prays that if a tragedy were to occur, let it be a *spectacular* tragedy—say, a fiery crash in an exotic car, or a heli-skiing miscalculation. Preferably captured on video.

Danny Doyle dons his duds and checks his mug in the mirror. His greatest disappointment in life so far is the cowlick that arcs over the left side of his brow in utter defiance of his comb. Because of the cowlick, he will never be cool. He is resigned.

"Cool is overrated," he advises his younger brothers, in passing. But, as he and the Doyle parents well know, the boys are collectively deaf to anything resembling common sense.

For a long moment, Danny considers his reflection. If he were said to have a sartorial style, it would be called *casual indifference*. He refuses to wear jeans, having read the medical reports that attribute sterility in men to the constricting nature of denim. No, his preference is a pair of loose-fitting khaki trousers. He also favours button-down shirts, or at least shirts with a collar of some description. He is unwilling to wear any article of clothing that advertises a fashion designer's name, or a rock band, or a corporation—at least, until those designers and rock stars and corporations agree to pay him for his advertising space. He wears white tennis shoes with three blue stripes down the sides. The overall effect is understated, subtle enough to avoid unnecessary attention. In high school, invisibility is a plus.

In the kitchen, the monkeys scuttle in, in ones and twos. They would swing from the chandelier if the paterfamilias wasn't present, lurking over a coffee, imagining the serenity of an isolated tropical island. The noise in the kitchen is impressive. Our man Dan, being closer in temperament to his father, sets a fine example at the other end of the table, calmly spooning cereal into his mouth. The chimps natter and spill each other's milk, while the woman of the house goes demonstrably insane, before which she will finish packing six lunches.

The morning ritual unfolds: limbs flail, bend in contrary ways; small objects sail across the table, threatening to put out an eye; enthusiastic elbows tip over juice jugs; hair is pulled and necks are pinched; fingers suffer painful monkey bites, prompting squeals of outrage and threats of retribution. Amid this chaos sit Danny and the senior Doyle, as if in a time warp, as if a trick of the camera creates the illusion they are playing out the scene in *slo-mo*, while the rest of the mob speeds headlong toward Keystone Kops posterity.

As the monkeys lower the benchmark of civilized human behaviour, Danny scans the discarded sections of his father's newspaper. He wants to be informed. At precisely ten minutes to eight, a lunch bag is deposited at his elbow with loving indifference; his mother has survived another morning rush hour, and Danny is on his way. The sudden tranquillity outside the front door is reassuring.

Danny Doyle does not take the bus to school. He has not done so since midway through the tenth grade, after he realized the ignominy of taking public transit was drawing attention from the more disreputable factions at Laidlaw High. He knows there are only three kinds of people in this world: predators, prey and chameleons, and Danny aims to fall squarely into the third category. He is not supported by a faction, except perhaps by the drama club.

Perhaps I give the misleading impression I am in the mainstream, but I am not. Like all artists, I am an outsider to the world at large— or at least to my own small part of a larger world. If I am loosely associated with the geeks at Laidlaw, it is because they, too, are outsiders, although of a different breed. They are geeks because they do not know how to conform. They can solve for x, but they lack the basic social skills and requisite cunning that would permit them to blend in, as I do. They are drawn to me because they see in me a kindred spirit, but I am not like them; I am a chameleon, they are prey. The only thing we have in common is that I, too, can solve for x.

Each weekday morning, after being consumed by a toxic blue haze as the bus thunders past, I wait on the corner for my best friend Raymond to arrive. I know that he will be late; he always is. I am resigned. After a brisk twenty-minute walk, we will arrive at school, moments before the second bell, late but not late. Because I am my father's son, I prefer to be early, so that I will have a few moments to settle matters at my locker and put my head into the right space for first class, which is Choir. Alas...

"Okay, c'mon, let's go," says Raymond, breathless, as if I am the one who is late. He doesn't even slow down. I have to take a few long strides to catch up.

"You're late," I say. Not a day goes by that I do not admonish him. Like a parent, I believe repetition will ultimately be effective. I am guardedly optimistic.

"It's not my fault," he says. Nothing ever is.

Raymond is an only child. His tardiness is inexcusable. His parents coddle and pamper him, lavish him with loving attention. I have no doubt they reserve prime morning bathroom time for their beloved fruit. There is no menagerie in his kitchen to tip over his bowl of Cheerios with a random lacrosse stick. He is permitted to smoke cigarettes in his bedroom, ostensibly because his parents foolishly believe that to deny him anything, to set limits of any kind, will only push him away, will cause him to take drugs or hide mickeys of Southern Comfort in his satchel. They don't want Raymond to have secrets. They are liberals.

"If you get up ten minutes earlier," I say, "we won't have to walk so fast."

"I like to walk fast."

"I like to walk fast, too, but not because I'm late."

"I slept through my alarm."

"Bullshit. You hit the snooze button."

"Maybe."

"Twice."

"Maybe."

"I've already told you how to solve this problem."

"What problem?"

"The problem of your being late every fucking morning."

"We're almost never late for class."

"That's not the point. We agreed to meet on the corner at eight o'clock, and you never get there until ten past."

"We're never late for class. Almost."

"You make me stand there, waiting for you. That's the point, Ray."

"Don't call me Ray."

"Put your alarm clock on the other side of the room. That way, you have to get out of bed to turn it off."

"Or hit the snooze button."

"Why would you hit the snooze button when you're already out of bed?"

"I could do it. No problem."

"Maybe you need to go to bed earlier. Obviously you're not getting enough sleep."

"Jesus, Danny, we're teenagers. There's no such thing as enough sleep."

"Nevertheless, I don't like having to wait for you every morning. My house is a goddamned zoo in the morning, and I manage to get out the door in time."

Raymond lights a cigarette. It's his way of changing the subject.

Raymond is Danny Doyle's best friend.

He is Danny Doyle's only friend. A handful of geeks will claim to be friends of Dado, but Dado will deny the charge. They are unilateral relationships. He tolerates acquaintances out of circumstantial necessity, but requires only one friend, and Raymond is it. It is a symbiotic relationship, with a clear hierarchy in which Danny ostensibly holds the reins of power. He does not believe in oligarchy, and democracy is, in his view, an unproven theory. There can only be one man in charge, and he is that man, controlling everything from their activities to their philosophy.

Take, for instance, their views on music, a subject on which Raymond is at great disadvantage, thanks to a tin ear.

"I like Nickleback," he says.

"No, you don't," says Danny.

"The video is cool."

"That doesn't make them a good band."

Raymond looks sceptical. "Okay, professor. What makes a good band, then?"

"The music. There is nothing else. You can't save a bad song with video."

"How do you explain Britney Spears?"

"Don't mention her name again in my presence, Ray."

"Don't call me Ray. There's nothing wrong with Nickleback, that's all I'm saying."

"They are tuneless deadbeats with nothing of interest to say, musically or otherwise. I'll bet you couldn't hum two bars of one of their songs."

Raymond makes the attempt, is derailed by his tin ear. Still, the tune is there, somewhere.

Dado will not be swayed. "Lucky guess. By this time next week your mind will be blank. Now, hum two bars of *Let it Be*."

Raymond tunelessly reproduces the bars.

"See what I mean? That melody is burned into your brain because it's a work of genius. Now, hum the opening bars to Beethoven's ninth symphony."

"This is stupid," says Raymond, who knows that he is out of his territory.

"Indulge me."

After rolling his eyes in exaggerated orbits, Raymond complies.

"I believe I've made my point," says Dado.

"Tell me again what the point is?" Although he gets fair grades, sometimes Raymond is slow on the uptake.

"The point is that today's music is devoid of artistic merit. A suit with an MBA sends a pretty girl to Pop Star school, where she learns to swivel her hips and mouth the words to some banal song, no doubt written by the MBA's fourteen-year-old girlfriend's cousin. Then the MBA spends four-hundred-thousand dollars producing a video that will be nothing but a licentious and inappropriate display of gyrating belly buttons and gaping halter-tops. The song is nothing without the belly button."

"I like the belly button."

"The belly button has nothing to do with the music. It's merely a way to trick impressionable children into buying an inferior product. A product, by the way, that is diluting an art, reducing it to a tasteless, homogenized pulp."

"Nickleback doesn't have any belly buttons in their video."

"You're missing the point, Ray. The artist has been removed from the decision-making process. Music is suffering a lingering death, and we're forced to listen to the pitiful squawks of that agonizing death. That's the point."

"Hm."

Danny Doyle possesses a prodigious musical ear that lacks only formal training and a modest amount of encouragement, neither of which is forthcoming. If it weren't for the oppressive nature of his harried parents—who are keen to squelch any ambition their children might harbour that will cost money and/or require being driven somewhere—he would already be an acknowledged genius.

"Take Choir," his pragmatic mother advised, clearly the source of Danny's genetic disposition toward cunning. "It's free, and you get a credit for it."

Danny acquiesced only because he knew that vocal chops would broaden his scope as a future actor. Keenly aware of the shortage in today's theatre scene of the *triple threat,* he has considered hitting up his parents for dance lessons; but if word got back to the factions at Laidlaw, he'd be dead.

It was destiny that brought Raymond Dunsmore and me together. Small-*d* destiny. On our first day at Laidlaw, he took the seat next to mine at the back of Mr. Bukowski's homeroom class. Laidlaw operates under the convenient system of alphabetization, so we were flung together by a letter. Our destiny as best friends was determined by our last names. Until that day, my best friend had been Elliot Manson. We were torn apart forever by the alphabet. Elliot's new best friend is Julian McKennally. Destiny.

As a male specimen of fourteen years, Raymond was physically underdeveloped when we met, but has since made some progress. At least he has no cowlick to rebel against him. But for that small detail, I do not envy him anything, not even his liberal parents, who should know better. He desperately wants to be cool, and will never succeed, in my opinion, solely because he is so desperate to be so.

"What do you think of this jacket?" he asks me. It is yellow, with a bold black logo spanning the back, plus a smaller rendering of the same logo on the front breast.

"How much did you pay for it?"

"Nothing. My mother bought it."

My mother will no longer buy me clothes, except for a few token items handed over on birthdays and at Christmas. Socks and undershirts. As the eldest child and burgeoning adult, I am expected to set an example for the younger ones by taking care of myself. I am being taught a lesson in independence, for which I am expected to be grateful.

"It's cool," I say, referring to Raymond's new jacket. Why should I contribute to my best friend's ultimate failure as a self-reliant adult?

"Yeah."

Raymond has not yet learned the value of a long hot shower. His squamous complexion puts off the girls of Laidlaw—admittedly superficial creatures who are incapable of seeing past the glowing pustules.

"You need a haircut," I remind him. Where is his mother?

"I'm growing a ponytail."

"Why?"

"I can't afford a motorcycle."

12

"Ponytails are déclassé."

"Huh?"

"If you want to be trailer trash, you should knock out a couple of teeth and buy yourself a Firebird."

"I wish I could afford a Firebird."

At moments like this, I question my own judgment, wonder if I wouldn't be better off with no friend at all. But if not for Raymond, my best friend might be one of the geeks, and that scenario would put me in grave danger. The jocks and the shop coolies relentlessly pick on the geeks. This is part of the natural order of things: predator and prey.

The Laidlaw factions are many and diverse, covering a broad cross-section of Toronto's cultural spectrum. The Gangbangers are much feared and routinely avoided, but they are a threat mainly to themselves, to their own inner factions, which are forever at war. They are too self-centered to concern themselves with outsiders. The Rockers are a grubby, ill-kempt lot, intimidating the weak-of-heart with a preponderance of damp leather and predictably bad haircuts. They are mostly harmless, unless they've been drinking. The Leslies represent the most violent, and the most foul-mouthed, of the female factions at Laidlaw. They are unpredictable and merciless in their efforts to debunk the traditional assertion that women are peace-loving creatures. If they can't find a suitable girl to accost, they have been known to molest a geek, taking his money and throwing him face-down in a mud puddle. The Goths and Vegans share a depressing predilection for black clothing, and an evangelical penchant for pasty makeup. Apart from the pierced body parts, the only thing separating them from the geeks is a long, hot bath and a shopping spree at Winners. The Skaters are appreciated solely for their entertainment value. The student body holds a collective breath, waiting for a skull to crack open on the concrete steps, another failed attempt to pull off a grinder. The Skids are ignored utterly by all, preparing them for the near future, when they become professional pan-handlers.

One day the coolies and jocks will get what's coming to them. I am convinced that the twenty-year high school reunion was a geek's idea. Two decades from now, the geeks of Laidlaw will be seven-figure tycoons, famous movie directors, internet moguls. They will arrive at the reunion in Porsches and Jaguars, with beautiful wives at their sides. All that money will not change the fact that they are geeks. They will continue to stutter, they will consider fart jokes the zenith of humour, their pants will be cinched a little too high on their waists, and their eyewear will be functional rather than fashionable. But they will be justifiably smug. This is the day they have lived for. No one, besides I, will match their success.

Several jocks will be shop stewards at the Ford plant. Many more will be in industrial sales, and will spend the entire evening trying to explain what that means. The rest will be politicians—an odious lot. Few of the coolies will attend the reunion. They will be in jail. The gangbangers will all be dead, and the rockers will be passed out drunk in a room at the Sandstone Hotel. The Leslies will be loving mothers in flower-print dresses, with faint scars on their shoulders and ankles, where the tattoos have been removed; they cannot deny their genetic heritage indefinitely. The goths will all be in advertising. They, like the politicians, will be pariahs at this event. The vegans will be living on a commune in the interior of British Columbia, and the skids will be slouched on a busy Queen Street sidewalk, begging smokes and quarters, sniffing glue. No one will know what became of the skaters.

Raymond is vulnerable only because he is trying to fit in, rather than blend in. I have repeatedly tried to explain the difference, to no effect. One of the primary obstacles preventing him from becoming cool is his name: Raymond. He resists all attempts to modify that rather mundane and awkward moniker. Raymundo, Ray Gun, X-Ray, Gamma Ray, Ray-O-Vac. Any of these alternatives might aide him in his pathetic bid to move up a notch on the cool meter. But he is unaccountably attached to his full, glorious birth name. This obstinacy is the result of a liberal upbringing, his parents are to blame.

I fear that we all grow up to be our parents. I have seen the evidence all around me. Take, for instance, the Millers, our neighbours across the street. They are long-standing members of the Church of Christ, a membership that makes them, in my father's view, fanatical crackpots. Still, my father's neighbourly conscience compels him to invite the Millers to our annual backyard barbecue, an event that has become an important and anticipated local tradition. It is regarded as the acme of the summer social season on our street. The Millers have never attended, and will not attend in the future, because alcohol is served and consumed at the event, which conflicts with their religious values. The Millers have a son, Neil, who is three years older than me. He has twice tried and failed to commit suicide. He started drinking at age twelve, and didn't stop until just last year. He dropped out of school after grade ten, tried to drink himself to death, failed, returned to school, was kicked out after one semester, was arrested for public drunkenness and disturbing the peace, was pulled to his feet by his concerned and loving parents, somehow managed to earn his diploma through correspondence, and has now enrolled in a fine arts program at a local college. His parents say he has "turned a corner" in his life. Neil has apparently turned to Jesus for guidance, returned to his parents' church, made peace with himself through the Lord Almighty. In other words, he has become his parents. Clearly, the corruptive influences of the outside world can take hold of us—booze, drugs, prime-time television, irrelevant pop music, friends with questionable morals—but, in the end, it is our parents who have the tightest grip on us. God help me.

I do what I can for my best friend, try to instil in him a more well-defined ideology than the left-wing hippie-dippy everything-is-beautiful doctrine served up by his parents, remind him that rules are a good thing, that without rules in life there will be bedlam. I demonstrate through example that personal and social responsibility is a vital skill that must be developed and crafted, if one is to succeed in life. I have had minor victories. He no longer watches *Friends* reruns religiously. He tucks his shirts in and wears a belt. He may have not yet fully embraced the work of artist Robert Rauschenberg, but he no longer claims it is "just some dirty old socks glued to the wall." I do what I can to fend off the formidable familial forces that threaten to stunt his development into a useful citizen. It is an uphill journey.

"If you want to be cool, you need a nickname, Ray."

"Don't call me Ray. My parents don't like it when you shorten my name. They say it's vulgar to give people nicknames."

"Your parents are not the best gauge for what is or isn't vulgar, Ray. Besides, all the cool people have nicknames. Shoeless Joe Jackson, Bugsy Segal, Tiny Tim."

Raymond gives me a sideways glance.

"Don't scoff. If it weren't for his nickname, Tiny Tim would be just another unemployed ukulele player."

"What about James Dean? He invented cool."

"Most people called him Jim. His close friends called him Jimmy or Jimbo or Deano. Or Blockhead."

"Blockhead?"

"He was nuts for auto racing. He was the only coolie who ever made it big."

"Hm."

"And Deano was cool, even with short hair."

"Times have changed."

I can't disagree with that.

As they walk, Dado must talk. Any lull in the conversation will be a void in Raymond's education. Dado feels tremendous pressure to fulfil his duty as best friend and mentor. Since they both are mere months away from attaining the privilege to vote, a new subject is introduced.

"Listen carefully, Ray."

Raymond listens. "I don't hear anything."

Danny punches him in the arm. "I haven't said anything, yet."

"Um."

"We're going to be voting for the first time, this year."

"Yeah?"

"We have to be on the lookout for a political party with a progressive mandate."

"What about the Conservative Party?"

"They're so far right, even the Bolsheviks consider them extremists. They couldn't have done worse if they'd hauled old Joe Clark out of the closet."

"Tell me again who Joe Clark is?"

"The guy with no chin."

"Right. The funny-looking guy."

Dado is pleased that his friend shows interest in the subject. He has made it clear to Raymond, in recent weeks, that a man is not entitled to complain about the government if he has not made the effort to cast an educated vote.

"Well, he's gone anyway. And it's not as if we need to like the guy for him to do a good job."

"Welcome to Reform Party politics, my friend. That sort of attitude will get you a deficit that your great-grandchildren will hate you for. Your statement has just killed forty-thousand senior citizens who no longer have a pension or affordable pharmaceuticals. You've just added five percent to the welfare rolls. Your pseudo-academic stance has just put us on an inexorable path toward civil war."

"I think you're overreacting."

16

"Listen. All we need is a leader who will make us *believe* that he knows how to lead."

"That seems a bit cynical."

"Let me ask you this. How do you feel when your mother is driving you somewhere?" Dado understands the value of the analogy.

Raymond shivers. "She's a terrible driver."

"Has she ever had an accident?"

"Not exactly. But she's had lots of close calls."

Dado nods. He has had several automotive experiences with Mrs. Dunsmore. "Why do you suppose that is?"

"She's nervous. She's always looking over her shoulder, except when she's changing lanes. Then she gets honked at by some dude she's just cut off, and that makes her even more nervous."

"And therein lies the point, Mister Gamma Ray. Even though she has a five-star rating, she gives the appearance of being incompetent. In politics, we prefer it the other way around. We need to have confidence in a politician, even if it's unwarranted, so that we can get on with our lives and not have to worry about what's really going on. Why do you think Americans have foisted so many actors into the political arena? They're perfect candidates. They're photogenic, they aren't afraid to speak to the crowds, and they don't meddle too much with the machinery. You might say, to use another automotive analogy, they want to steer the thing, but they aren't really interested in looking under the hood to see how it works."

Raymond frowns.

"My point is, with the conservatives in power, your girlfriend will have to take the bus to Buffalo to get an abortion."

"I don't have a girlfriend."

"Say good-bye to Sunday shopping, say hello to no-fault insurance."

"I don't have insurance."

"Say good-bye to speeches, say hello to sermons."

"Hello, sermon."

We are getting close to school. Raymond lights another cigarette. "It's all a bit confusing." He exhales and brushes an ash off the black logo on his breast. "I'm not going to know who to vote for, when the time comes."

I must wrap things up for now, but I am not through with the subject. I will persist until I am confident he will make the right decision. "Just consider this. The current government is renovating our prisons, tearing down the ugly cinderblock cells and putting up cosy little cottages, nestled in the trees. Murderers and pimps will be incarcerated in these cottages as punishment for their crimes."

"That doesn't seem right."

"I saw it on the news. They're giving them cottages."

"Jesus."

"Do your parents have a cottage?"

Raymond shakes his head. "They can't afford it."

"Nor can mine. But our tax dollars are buying some arsonist a five-year vacation in one. It's an outrage. I'm giving serious consideration to a life of crime. It seems to pay off nicely, if you manage to get caught."

Raymond raises a sceptical eyebrow.

"Why should I go through the trouble of getting a university education, then spending the next twenty years building a career, just so I might one day afford a cottage, when all I have to do is kill someone or sell some crack, and I can have the cottage right away, free of charge?"

"I see what you mean."

"Once the gangbangers find out about the cottages, we'll see a crime spree like never before. Mark my words."

The second bell is ringing as Raymond flicks his cigarette butt into the flowerbed, and we enter the front door. Another day at Laidlaw High has begun.

Chapter 2

After homeroom, Raymond and I will be separated until lunchtime. We sit at the back of the classroom, for reasons obvious to any chameleon, where we are free to converse quietly for twenty minutes, until we are accounted for and move on to first class. Our schedules intersect only for Mrs. Stock's afternoon English class. My friend and I are taking different routes to academic glory. I will learn advanced algebra while he plays dodge-ball in the gymnasium. I have given him fair warning about athletic pursuits, but he is resolute.

"Now that Chip Healy's knee is gone, the coach says I'm in line for second string," Raymond whispers, as Mr. Bukowski, our homeroom teacher, takes roll call.

"So what?" I take great pride in my expansive lack of sporting knowledge.

"That means I may actually get to play in a game."

"I told you not to join the team. Basketball is for troglodytes. You're better than that, Ray."

"I like it."

"Tell me one good thing about it."

"Chicks."

"Wasn't the ponytail supposed to solve that problem?"

"If you had zits, you'd understand."

"There are easier ways to attract girls than joining the basketball team."

"Like what?"

I ignore the question. This is an old argument. "I just don't see why it had to be basketball."

"I wanted to try out for football, but Coach Fenchurch told me not to bother."

"I was thinking more along the lines of tennis. If you have to take a sport, at least tennis is civilized. Tennis is a gentleman's game. There's no contact involved."

"We don't have a tennis team."

"You should have joined the swim team, then. It's better exercise than basketball and you're less likely to get your arm broken."

"Can't. I'm allergic to chlorine. Besides, they practice at six in the fucking morning."

"What about volleyball?"

"Only for the girls."

"You should have dropped gym last year."

"Marion Dalton is on the cheerleading squad."

We take a moment to admire Marion. She sits near the front, a calculated strategy. She is well aware of her status as the most desirable girl in school. I am briefly sad for Raymond. She is so far out of his league, he will never even have a conversation with her, let alone make a pass. Some things are simply foregone, unchangeable. I stand a better chance of bringing home a Super Bowl ring than he does, scoring with Marion Dalton. If only my friend would lower his expectations to a more realistic level, he might stand a chance of scaling the north face of K4, or finding a cure for cancer. Set realistic goals, I tell him.

I refuse to devote the time to wish for things I can never have. I acknowledge Marion Dalton's superior beauty, but set my bar at a surmountable height. I have cast my hopes on Heidi Borland. We are in the drama club together.

Heidi hasn't finished growing into her features, but I can see the future, and one day she will be spectacular. She will be a late bloomer. Because she is not yet fully formed, she is invisible to the popular boys at Laidlaw. Only the geeks and I recognize her potential. Even Heidi cannot imagine what she will become, the caterpillar who doesn't know she will soon be a butterfly.

My progress with Heidi has been slow. My lack of experience and her ambivalence do not help. She is taciturn, aloof, guarded, and works nearly as hard to deflect amorous attention as Marion Dalton works to get it. I know that if I were to ask Heidi, she would tell me she thinks Marion Dalton degrades herself, and her gender, by using her stunning good looks to manipulate those around her. Heidi believes that true love can never result from such a shallow tactic. She dreams

20

of finding a man who will love her soul, and she is convinced that that man does not exist at Laidlaw, that high school boys are too immature to see beyond the surface. I will change her mind, I am utterly confident.

As for the geeks, they, like Raymond and his futile infatuation with Marion Dalton, are deluding themselves. Even Heidi Borland is out of their reach.

While I dream of Heidi, Marion, sensing an appreciative gaze, turns her head and meets my eye before I can turn away. Her eyes narrow, pass down a judgment on me that amounts to indifference. I am merely another redundant affirmation of her beauty. I have nothing to lose by being caught staring. I am one of a thousand anonymous admirers who ogle her all day long.

It would be unprecedented for me, or any chameleon, to date Marion Dalton. But leaving aside for a moment the peril of drawing attention to myself by consorting with a "popular" girl, I know that Marion would be a disappointing companion. Like Raymond, I have never had a conversation with her, but I am an inveterate eavesdropper. She giggles in a way that causes my scrotum to contract. We could never have a meaningful discussion about anything that wasn't related to the quantum application of makeup. I fear she would expect me to go shopping with her at the mall, during which she will complain endlessly about her many best friends, and about her ongoing battle against fly-aways. "It's the humidity," I will explain. "If you don't want fly-aways, you'll have to move to a drier climate." She will take offence to my sensible answer. "Don't be a jerk, Danny. I'm trying to tell you something important." I will promptly leap over the Level 3 railing, sail gracefully through the shopping din, a background layer of Neil Diamond, plummet to my death rather than spend another second with this vacuous doll.

We are locked in a battle of wills, Marion and I. She taunts me by raising the corner of her fine mouth almost imperceptibly, parting her glossed lips, exposing the strawberry crest of her tongue. I detect her disappointment as I fail to perspire. She redoubles her attack by casually flicking her hair with her hand. I will not crack. Raymond is riveted by our duel, no doubt mad with jealousy, presumably taking measure of my fortitude, assimilating my impressive technique. Marion moves in for the kill, twisting subtly in her chair, arching her back. The shot goes wide and I parry with an eye roll that puts an end to our little exchange. Marion's eyes return to the front of the class and Raymond pats me heartily on the shoulder. For a brief moment, I fear he will applaud.

"Way to go, Danny. She likes you."

I brush his hand away. "Don't be a fool. I just spared you a lot of grief." Raymond will not appreciate what I have done for him until many years have passed and he is happily married to a sensible girl.

"I wish my hair grew faster."

"Make sure your mother takes a few pictures of your ponytail when it finally grows in," I tell him. My prescience informs me that Raymond, by the time he has reached the age of thirty, will have the smoothest, shiniest pate at the insurance company where he will surely be employed. He will appreciate the photographs of his youthful ponytail, a kind reminder, in his middle-life, that he was once capable of growing such a specimen. And he will not feel as badly about his balding head when he sees the historic evidence of the rampant acne that once afflicted him so severely. I decide at this moment to harass my friend no more about his proposed ponytail, permit him this small future joy. I am resigned.

"Here," whispers Raymond.

"What?"

He points toward the front of the class, where Mr. Bukowski sits and takes roll call.

"Daniel Doyle," says Mr. Bukowski, evidently for the second time.

"Here," I say.

Mr. Bukowski lives in my neighbourhood, and he is a Jehovah's Witness. I know these two facts about him because he has stood on my doorstep in a grey suit, gripping a leather briefcase.

I wasn't surprised that he didn't seem to recognize me when I answered the door. Mr. Bukowski's mind has a tenuous connection to the real world, not unlike many religious zealots. Before I discovered he was a Jehovah's Witness, I attributed his seemingly delicate condition to a twenty-year stretch as a high school teacher. After peering through the screen door at him as he cradled a copy of Watchtower magazine in his free arm, I understood his detachment. When he isn't taking attendance for the D's, he is psyching himself up for an afterlife that will surely be an improvement over the current one—presumably one without teenagers.

In my ability to discourage holy personnel from disrupting my household's Saturday afternoon routine, I am still an apprentice. Already that morning I thwarted a pair of apple-cheeked Mormons and nimbly deflected a persistent canvasser for the Wildlife Fund (a different sort of religion, my father says). When I recognized my homeroom teacher, I felt I should not contend with this intruder; I had a conflict of interest. Besides, the Jehovah's Witnesses are rated among the most difficult to repel. The Master had to be called in for this one.

"Dad! It's for you!"

I hovered at the other end of the foyer, where I could observe and learn.

My father's heavy footsteps broadcast his irritation, and his silhouette soon blocked the daylight in the open door. The screen door remained the only obstacle protecting my family from salvation.

"What do you want?"

I recoiled slightly at his tone of voice. I have been on the receiving end of that tone enough times in my life that I experienced a curious urge to clean my room.

"Are you familiar with our magazine?" said Mr. Bukowski. His voice was thin, tremulous, weak. I recognized it, but I was not used to hearing him speak in full sentences. I had never heard him say anything other than a name beginning with the letter *d*. "There's a timely article that your family might enjoy called The Bible's Power in Your Life—"

"What are you selling?" This always stumps them.

"I beg your pardon?"

"Are you selling something?"

"Um, no, there's nothing to buy. Watchtower magazine is yours for free. If you'd like some time to read the issue, I can come back in a week and we can talk about it."

My father ignored the proffered magazine. He knows that once you take the goods, they've got you. "Why are you here?"

Mr. Bukowski did not know how to respond. "Are you familiar with our mag—"

"You must be selling something," said my father. "Otherwise, you wouldn't be disturbing me on my day off."

"There's nothing to buy. It's just—"

"God?"

"I beg your pardon?"

"You're selling God?"

"One doesn't sell God. One embraces Him, in all His glory. One lives through His word. One—"

"Okay, listen." He was about to terminate the meeting. I surmised by this that the golf was a close match, he was anxious to get back to it. "If I want a chicken, I'll go to a supermarket. If I want a car, I'll go to a dealership. And if I want God, I'll go down to a goddamned church and pick one up. If you've got a chicken in that briefcase, I'll pay a fair price for it. Otherwise, fuck off and leave us alone. You're traumatizing my children." He slammed the door in the face of my homeroom teacher, turned to face me, winked, and shuffled back to the sofa. I assimilated the lesson and prayed to God that Mr. Bukowski did not recognized me.

Now that he has vanquished Marion Dalton, Dado is feeling good about the day. An extra ten minutes under the hot shower nozzle has pressed his cowlick into rare submission; his hair looks particularly dapper today. He is wearing his favourite Eddie Bauer shirt, which has finally emerged from the laundry room after languishing in the dirty pile for over a week. His mother is further behind schedule than usual. And today, being Monday, is drama club, so he will be in his finest form at the end of the day, when he sees Heidi Borland.

Danny Doyle's ear suddenly explodes with exquisite pain.

"Ow!"

His fingers come away from the ear with small traces of blood. Two rows over, he spots Frank Dolan. His nemesis. Frank has no affiliation with the factions of Laidlaw High. He is a free-agent bully. Only an independent bully would pick on a chameleon.

Frank Dolan still has the rubber band wound round his fingers, and a small pile of paper clips on the desk at his elbow. He openly takes credit for the assault, mocking Danny by flipping his hair and licking his lips seductively. He evidently witnessed the exchange with Marion Dalton.

Despite the searing pain in his ear, Dado yawns. It is his only defence against a man with three inches and thirty pounds on him. Rumour has it Frank was invited to try out for the football team, but politely declined the offer, ostensibly because it would have interfered with his tyrannical métier. He takes his violent craft seriously.

For a bully, Frank Dolan is uniquely intelligent. He takes

advanced algebra with Danny Doyle. He takes Chemistry with Danny Doyle. The very fact he has chosen Danny Doyle as a favourite among a select group of victims demonstrates a superior mind is at work. But Frank has embraced the dark side—like Holmes's diabolical foe, Moriarty—squandering his intelligence on the nefarious enterprise of terrorizing the innocent.

What Dado understands about Frank Dolan is this: he is lonely. He is an outsider who could easily gain acceptance in one of the milder factions, if only he would make a positive effort. Instead, he must lash out, employing headlocks and arm twists, bumping shoulders in the hallways, stamping on feet, tipping over lunch trays, extracting cash fees and confiscating personal items, and generally being a nuisance, as a way of endearing himself. He can't imagine any way of making a friend other than through these ruthless methods. Because he is miserable, he must make others miserable.

If he was not so busy setting Raymond straight, Danny Doyle might attempt to steer Frank Dolan onto a more productive track. Alas, with only a few months left before they are all ejected into a cruel world, there is only so much Dado can accomplish. He does not want to spread himself too thin. Frank will have to sort out his own problems.

Raymond has seen what happened. "Just say the word and I'll get the team to break every bone in Frank's body."

"Thanks anyway," says Danny. He knows that Raymond is still trying to justify his athletic aspirations. "I'd be happier if you clubbed him senseless with a tennis racquet or snapped him in the thigh with a wet towel, but I sense I'm talking to a brick wall."

"Pretty much, yeah."

The 8:50 bell sounds, signalling the end of roll call, and the start of my transition to first period, which, as I've said, is Choir. My ear still throbs, but I am ready. My day is about to begin.

Chapter 3

As I stride out of homeroom, ear still blazing, Frank follows close behind. I don't know he is there until he speaks.

"Do I bore you, *Boyle?*" One of his pet names for me.

I don't look back. With five younger brothers, I have learned that if you ignore pests, they will often go away. Children are like that: they just want attention, and if they can't get it from me they will seek it elsewhere. I give credit to Frank for sheer tenacity.

"I wouldn't want to *bore* you, Boyle. That's the thing."

"Shut up, Frank," says Ray, who walks beside me.

Ray is no coward, but he is justifiably wary of Frank. In any case, my friend is turning right, where lies Remedial Math, in the west wing. He says his piece and makes his escape. I refuse to alter my step in order to leave behind this irritation. I have spent too much time and effort developing a stride that will exude modest confidence and purpose, thus encouraging others to pay me no mind. Sometimes it works.

I have made a careful study of the way others walk, and my conclusion is that a person's gait will either call attention to him or it will deflect attention away. The geeks, for instance, walk too quickly and tend to bob up and down, as if the tendons in their ankles are strung too tightly. The gangbangers are forced to shuffle at a snail's pace due to the baggy pants that hang indecently below their waists, gathering at the knees. How they ever outrun the police I will never know. The rockers have, without question, the worst posture. Their shoulders slope forward, their scruffy heads lolling perilously from thin necks, ready to drop off and roll away—a loss anyone would be hard-pressed to notice. The coolies lurch from side to side, giving them a tendency to bump into others in the crowded hallways. Brief scuffles occur daily due to this, but I have determined that it is, for the most part, unintentional. Coolies are uncomfortable walking anywhere; it is only when they are *driving* that they feel at home. The Leslies waddle in unison, as if burdened with full diapers, wearing threatening expressions that dare comment. I have modelled my own stride after the jocks, who stand erect and are more in tune with their bodies. I keep a steady pace and wear the demeanour of someone who knows, at all times, exactly where he is going.

"What's the hurry, Boyle? Can't wait to get your dress on so you can sing with the girls?" Frank knows my schedule by heart. He is thorough.

I maintain an even stride and a cool head, and concentrate on making myself invisible. Literally.

Dado has always believed that one day he will do it: make himself vanish. As evidence that he is not insane, he has never told anyone about this belief; not even Raymond. He comprehends the fundamental science of the universe. He even has a basic grasp of quantum physics, which he will not study in earnest until he moves on to university. Yet, because he understands so much of this world, he knows there are many more things he does not understand. He knows, for instance, that two-hundred years ago, few men would have believed it was possible to fly. He knows that sixty years ago, many men would have scoffed at the notion of travelling to the moon. Just because we don't know how, thinks Dado, doesn't mean it's not possible. It's only a matter of concentration.

Not long ago, I nearly succeeded. I was alone in my room, practicing, when I became briefly transparent. It lasted only for a few seconds, but I swear I could see the bedspread through my legs. I have been unable to duplicate the feat, but I have utter confidence that with time I shall do it. I fear it will not happen at this moment, when it would be especially convenient. Frank Dolan is still on my tail.

"*Hosanna* Boyle. That's what I'm going to call you from now on."

In a few short years, after I have become a world-famous actor, Frank will tell his fellow inmates that he used to be best friends with the great Danny Doyle.

"If I had a nickel," I say, over my shoulder, "I'd buy you a friend."

His response is to step on my left heel and push me forward. I fall to the ground, scattering my morning books across the floor. Passers-by trod on my papers and keep moving, offering nothing in the way of help. It's the least a chameleon can expect. I look up at Frank. He is laughing, kicking my notebooks farther down the hall. My left shoe is off, mutilated. When I reach for the shoe, Frank toes it away. It gets kicked twice more by others—unintentionally, I think. Frank is nearly done with me, for now. One quick punt to my thigh and he is ready to move on to his first class, which is French. I know his schedule as well as he knows mine. Information-gathering is part of a solid defence.

I fetch my shoe and my books, hobble to the music room. Most of my classmates are already there, and none asks why I am limping. Only after I have sat down do I notice that my sock is torn and my heel is bleeding. There is a two-inch scrape, underscored by the white flap of skin that was peeled away.

When he notices a button missing from his favourite Eddie Bauer shirt, Danny Doyle silently makes this vow: "Before the day is through, I will have revenge upon Frank Dolan."

I am a tenor.

Being a good tenor will get me better parts in the Broadway musicals. A halfway decent bass will end up in the chorus. I have trained my voice well. The overriding downside to being a tenor manifests itself outside the music room. A tenor, even a good tenor, has a speaking voice that falls somewhat into a weak grey area. *Basso* is preferable when one is attempting to exert authority. My father is a fine example of this. When he has something to say, people tend to listen. Even a bass-baritone would carry more weight than a tenor. I fear it is now too late to retrain my vocal apparatus.

Like any young man of uncertain confidence, I had originally wanted to be in the bass section, to shape my developing vocal apparatus into those deep, manly tones. On my first day at Laidlaw, at age fourteen, I could have gone either way. My voice had recently cracked, and hadn't yet decided how it was going to settle. Mr. Seale made the decision for me, announcing with no apparent forethought that I would sit in the tenor section. My protests fell upon deaf ears. Like Mr. Bukowski, Mr. Seale is a twenty-year man. He has impressive defence mechanisms. Now, three years later, I am resigned.

Few of my classmates possess even a trace of genuine musical aptitude. The alto section, in particular, would suffer little if my tuneless friend Raymond were to join their ranks. At times, I am forced to stretch my vocal limits to help those hopeless girls with their futile attempts at musicality, abandon my own section in an effort to prop up a weaker element. I try to lead them back into 4/4 time, demonstrate the simplicity of eight successive quarter notes, followed by a whole-note rest, round them up like wandering sheep and shepherd them back in the direction of the song at hand. The thanks I get for this extra effort is censure from Mr. Seale.

"Mister Doyle," he shouts, stopping us midway through the song. "You're singing the wrong part."

"I'm singing the wrong part *correctly*," I say.

"Do I need to show you how to read the tenor's part, Mister Doyle?" Formality is insisted upon in the music room.

"I know how to read the tenor's part, sir."

"Evidently you don't. You were singing the alto's part."

"Someone had to, sir."

"Yes, Mister Doyle. They are called altos, and they are the ones who traditionally sing the alto's part. You, sir, are a tenor, which explains why you are sitting in the tenor section. If you look closely, Mister Doyle, you should be able to detect what it is that distinguishes a tenor from an alto."

I look at the alto section. "Talent?"

Several sopranos titter.

"*Breasts*, Mister Doyle. They have breasts." The bass and baritone sections explode with laughter. I could have pointed out several altos who failed to measure up in that area, too, but held my tongue. "Wishful thinking on your part, perhaps, Mister Doyle?" He smiles faintly.

I am surrounded by bullies.

"Perhaps your neighbour, Mister Gillespie, can point to the correct spot on the page for you."

Gillespie begins to sweat. He will blame me for getting him drawn into the fray. He sits beside me because he, too, relies on my skill to guide him. He is a weak singer who cannot read music, and no amount of tutelage will change either fact. Poor Gillespie would have better luck translating ancient haiku into Esperanto than he would reading four bars of *Jesu Joy of Man's Desiring*. He can barely read the English alphabet. He is illiterate, as well as tone deaf. Poor fucker. He doesn't know that Mr. Seale is being sarcastic.

"Um—" says Gillespie. He fumbles with his sheet music and the pages slide off the stand.

"From the beginning," says Mr. Seale. He stands behind the grand piano and pounds the keyboard like a honky-tonk hack.

Too many years of instructing hopeless and ungrateful teenagers has stripped away Mr. Seale's love of music. Two decades ago, he must have had high hopes of instilling in those children his vast knowledge and sharing his appreciation for the art of music. He must have dreamt of discovering, along the way, a prodigy or two that he could lay claim to as a mentor. I am not aware of a single prodigy ever having passed through the halls of Laidlaw High. Our sports teams have never won a championship. The trophy case in the front foyer has a dusty plastic flower arrangement in it. Our highest academic achievers go on to become mediocre college professors, but do not get nominated for the Nobel Prize. Even the most talented shop coolies will never make it to the Daytona 500, except as spectators.

If his heart had still been in it, Mr. Seale might have taken me under his wing, nurtured me, molded my raw talent into a vocal force. But he has stagnated. His primary interest, now, is in humiliating his male students at every convenient opportunity, and making inappropriately suggestive remarks to, or about, those girls who possess well-developed endowments. It is always cold in the music room—a tactic he uses in order to make the girls' nipples expand. At the beginning of each year, he gives a forty-minute speech to the new class, outlining the course objectives, and detailing the many rules that govern the music room. In the midst of this speech, in which he bans chewing gum and coffee, he casually mentions that, "While tight pants can be a lesser problem, restraining garments on or around the torso can cause unfortunate and painful restrictions. This comment," he says, "is directed primarily at the girls in the room, those who are inclined to wear brassieres."

The natural solution to this problem, he goes on to explain, is for these girls to refrain from wearing such restrictive garments, in his class at least. He makes it perfectly clear that this is not a requirement, but that failure to comply might have an impact on a student's grade, since a student's grade is based on that student's ability to perform. "Naturally, any singer whose chest and diaphragm are able to move freely will outperform one who is fettered by these offensive garments." When the boys in the class hear this part of the speech, they invariably feel better about letting their mothers talk them into taking Choir. Some of them cheer. He's a sly one, old Mr. Seale.

By the twelfth grade, most of the girls have resumed wearing their brassieres. I imagine sooner or later their mothers find out about Mr. Seale's speech and annul his depraved guidance.

One notable exception is Lydia Henshaw. She, in particular, requires the support of a bra more than the other girls, yet she is determined to get a good grade. She is the most hopeless of all the altos. She has had an embarrassing crush on me for two years, and even her obvious ripeness cannot persuade me to see her as a romantic prospect. Last year, when we were required to pair off for our duets— an exercise worth an alarming twenty-five percent of our grade—she nearly knocked down three people in order to get to me first. Frankly, they weren't exactly lining up at my door. In spite of my talent, I am generally overlooked by my peers, except by Lydia. "Hi, Danny," she said, standing over me, breathless, braless, desperate.

She has had a bum rap at Laidlaw because it is rumoured that she is epileptic. Whether or not the rumour is true is irrelevant to the superstitious peasants that comprise the student body. A hundred years ago, their ancestors would have set the poor girl alight, crossing themselves to ward off the evil eye as she went up in smoke. My classmates are afraid to touch her in case she is contagious. They do not want to be sitting next to her in the cafeteria when she begins to convulse, swallows her tongue, turns a deep shade of magenta before expiring in her poutine. I happen to know something about epilepsy, and I am not afraid of it; nor am I afraid of Lydia for having it—if the rumour is true. No, it is her overwhelming desperation that turns me off. Such behaviour is expected of teenage boys, but I find the quality repugnant in a girl.

Later, when I complained to Raymond, he was typically unsympathetic.

"She's not bad," he said. "I'd do her. Nice tits."

"Is that how you judge the merits of a woman?" At least I have exorcised my friend's epileptic superstitions.

"Sure. What else is there?"

"You're pathetic."

"She likes you, and she has nice tits. What more do you want?"

"A smattering of brain cells would be nice. Someone who can

carry on a conversation without mentioning the cast of *Gossip Girl.*
Someone who doesn't giggle unless there is something actually funny
to giggle at. Someone with intelligent ideas and meaningful opinions
about life and the world. Pay attention, Ray, or you'll wind up
marrying a girl like Lydia."

"Jesus, Danny. Who's getting married? We're teenagers. I don't
know about you, but I just want to get laid."

"You make it sound like a contest."

"Imagine the humiliation of turning eighteen and still being a
virgin."

"The horror," I say.

In ninety-two days, Dado will turn eighteen. He is still a virgin.
Unless he makes some fast progress with Heidi Borland, there is little
hope that he will meet the deadline. The humiliation will be his.

Raymond has already achieved his objective. Last spring, with
Danny's reluctant approval, he pursued Lydia Henshaw until she
agreed to go out with him. It wasn't much of a pursuit. All he had to
do, in the end, was ask.

"You'll be sorry," Danny said. But he understands that people
need to make their own mistakes in order to learn from them.

Raymond just grinned.

"Congratulations, Ray," said Dado, after he learned of his friend's
copulative triumph.

"Don't call me Ray."

"How can you bear to spend time with her? What do you talk
about?"

Raymond shrugged.

As a couple, they lasted only three months. Once school let out
for the summer, Lydia went north to spend the summer vacation at
her family cottage, to Raymond's great relief.

"She was too possessive. My mother complained about all the
phone calls."

"Phone calls?"

"She'd call me up, even if I'd just left her house, and she'd talk for
an hour and a half."

"What on earth could she talk about for an hour and a half?"

"Beats me. Most of the time, I was playing Nintendo. I swear I
could put the receiver down for ten minutes, and when I'd pick it back

up, there she'd be...*blah blah blah*. She took twenty minutes just to say good-bye."

"I believe my next line is 'I told you so,'" said Dado.

"Anyway, I got laid. That's all that matters."

I believe I am the only senior at Laidlaw who has not had a sexual experience. The geeks don't count; most of them will be virgins until their thirties. I have never had a girlfriend. I have had two dates, with two different girls, and they were both disasters. I have often heard it said that girls mature faster than boys, but I have seen no evidence of this. I cannot lower myself to pursue the Laidlaw girls just to satisfy a physical urge, no matter how demanding that urge may be. I am convinced that, for me, manual love is preferable to affiliating myself with one of these brainless creatures. Except Heidi Borland. She is unique among her peers. She is my Destiny. Capital *D*.

Our first meeting was inauspicious.

Mrs. Banks runs the drama club at Laidlaw. By day she teaches psychology, which amounts to spending ten months repeatedly explaining the difference between the id, the ego and the superego. I am not a Freudian, so I dropped the course after grade nine, choosing instead to investigate the subject independently, through the school library. I began my self-tutelage with a 500-page text called *Personality Disorders and the Five-Factor Model of Personality*. The title portends a clinical verbosity that fails to disappoint. It has been an invaluable resource for helping me cope with my family, who do not, for the most part, grant me the respect I am due. This year I discovered *Advanced Abnormal Psychology*. It was the title that intrigued me; I needed to know if *Advanced* referred to the psychological or the abnormal aspect of the subject. It was on the shelf next to *Abnormal Psychology*. Surely, no one in his right mind would take the latter, when the former so clearly promises an *Advanced* study. I am halfway through my second pass at the text, and I have not been able to figure out what is wrong with me, exactly, but I am narrowing down the field. I surreptitiously removed all three books from the library shelf and stuffed them into my satchel. It is irresponsible of the school to have such information at the disposal of teenagers, who are already inclined to act in bizarre and unpredictable ways. Books such as these will only put bad ideas into susceptible minds. I will get no thanks, once again, for a good deed.

The drama club is my only means of contact with Heidi Borland. She is new to Laidlaw this year and, as luck would have it, I have no classes with her. If the school board had not phased out grade thirteen, I might have legally changed my last name to Bowman, so that I might spend an extra twenty minutes in the same room with Heidi in homeroom. Alas.

We were thrust together ten minutes after meeting. Mrs. Banks called on us to read a scene from *Taming of the Shrew*. The exercise was designed to give Mrs. Banks an indication of our acting abilities, from which she could more effectively cast us in the spring production of *Romeo and Juliet*. Mrs. Banks is a nut for Shakespeare. Our cold read brought the house down, as they say, and equal credit must be given to Heidi, who held up her end of the text magnificently.

"You were really good up there," I whispered, sidling up to her on the downstage floor, where we watched the others take their turn. She nodded away my praise without even making eye contact. She also failed to return the compliment, an oversight that I attributed to shyness. When I realized I had used a weak adjective and coupled it with a lame adverb, I backtracked. "You were compelling." Much better.

She *shushed* me.

I decided then and there that she was a disagreeable elitist. Nevertheless, I couldn't take my eyes off her. I was smitten. Heidi is dark in the same way that Marion Dalton is light. One is the colour of milky tea, while the other is a shaft of May sunlight. I am drawn to the dark side.

When Leonard Mapother and Donna Sanderson finished their scene, Heidi looked at me. "I love that scene," she said.

I nodded. If I attempted to say anything, I would have been no better than Lydia Henshaw in my desperation.

We have had a minimalist relationship since that first awkward day. A brief sentence or two, a nod, a shrug, any vague gesture. We are giving ourselves up one drop at a time, holding back the flood of emotions that would surely lead to a Great Love. We tease each other by withholding, denying the other satisfaction. It is a complicated game with many unspoken rules. It reminds me of the game my siblings play, where they look into each other's eyes and try not to blink; whoever blinks first, loses the game. My eyes are wide open.

I see Heidi in the hallways between classes. Like me, she has a purposeful stride and a faraway gaze that gets her to next class unmolested. Every day I see her in the lunchroom. She sits with a group, though it is never the same group two days in a row, and I am not even sure if she knows each group. I have not seen her talk to any of them. She does not contribute to their conversations, although she listens with seeming interest. I cannot approach her in the lunchroom because she is surrounded by these strangers. I am afraid to ask her out on a date because I know she will say no, even if she wants to say yes. The game is strict, cruel, thrilling.

It has happened again. Dado realizes too late that he has once again been looking at one girl but thinking about another. From across the music room, Lydia Henshaw has caught him staring at her. She smiles desperately and continues to screech the vague melody to some other song. Danny Doyle blinks, then rubs his eyes. He does not wish to encourage the girl. He shifts his gaze back to the music in front of him. Gillespie reaches over and points to the correct spot on the page.

Chapter 4

I entered the workforce at an early age, not by choice. My father does not believe in giving his children allowance, and, in a rare display of solidarity, my mother agrees with him. As the eldest Doyle child, it naturally fell to me to attempt to reason with my miserly parents. But in any family structure, reason tends to flow in only one direction.

"The fundamental skills of money management are developed in childhood," I told them. "If you expect your sons to learn to be financially responsible *after* they graduate from university, you'll pay a steep price when they fail to make it on their own, and move back home." I was speaking on behalf of the monkeys. I am confident of my own future success, in spite of parental negligence.

"Don't be melodramatic, Daniel," said my mother.

"I'm doing you a favour by bringing this up before it's too late. Give us the means to learn the proper handling of money and ten years from now you'll have the bathroom to yourselves every morning. You two lovebirds can enjoy a luxurious, peaceful breakfast together. No more paper-bag lunches to prepare. No more truck-loads of laundry each week. You'll be free to watch the Arts & Entertainment channel any time you like. Think of it." I gave them a moment to think of it. "As it is, we'll never be equipped to survive on our own. You'll sail into your golden years towing a bickering mob of needy, middle-aged freeloaders."

"Can it, Danny," said my father. "Do something useful around here and I might give you a quarter."

He'll never get to Bermuda with that attitude.

"I cut the grass, the other day."

"You and the boys play out there. Why shouldn't you cut the grass?" His logic was mystifying.

At the age of twelve, I began cutting neighbourhood lawns at ten dollars a go. By fourteen, I had talked my way into an entry-level position at Kelso's department store. I was vague about my age, and easily impressed the assistant manager with my maturity and enthusiasm. I received two evening shifts during the week and a full shift on Saturdays, giving assistance to whichever department required my generic talents. I was a stock boy. Naturally, I was soon resented by the other stock boys for my hard work and gumption. They were, one and all, lazy oafs who will never experience the satisfaction of a job well done. Apparently my *vim* made them look bad.

I spent more than three years at Kelso's, performing my duties laudably in every sector, from ladies' shoes to kitchenware. I was instrumental in reorganizing the stereo displays so that the products were arranged according to value rather than brand name, initiating a quantifiable boost in sales for the department. I could unload a shipment of winter coats, and still have time to locate a cheese grater for an inquiring customer. I could sweep up a chemical spill in the plumbing aisle and retag a candy display without breaking a sweat. My loyalty and hard work were rewarded, this past December, with a pink slip inserted into my pay envelope. I have only recently acquired my social insurance card, and I am already a victim of corporate downsizing. The assistant manager would not meet my gaze as I strode out of Kelso's for the last time. Kelso's has lost not only one of its most valuable employees, but also a valued customer. I will not shop there again.

On the upside, I have managed to save almost all of my Kelso earnings. I have over three thousand dollars in an interest-bearing savings account. No thanks to my parents.

My father sells radio airtime. I am sorry for him. He wanted to become a rock 'n' roll deejay, but his parents threatened him with immediate and irrevocable "independence" if he did not enrol in college to study business.

Popular music was only one of the many things my grandparents were against. Foreign-made cars were a treasonous attempt to undermine the moral underpinnings of a society that was already, in their view, hemorrhaging values—the result, apparently, of a generation of long-haired boys sunk in a haze of drugs, who harboured American draft-dodgers and impregnated decent girls. Cigarettes and alcohol were taboo. My aunt was not permitted to wear pants. Pets were banned from the household as carriers of unnamed but invariably fatal diseases. My father tells me these things as a way of illustrating how easy and comfortable my journey through childhood has been. He waits impatiently for my undying gratitude. But when I was twelve he promised to one day take me to Disney World. I can wait as long as he can to have my expectations fulfilled.

As for my disapproving grandparents, I never met them. Henry Doyle was an architect and painter who never measured up in either field. He married badly, selecting the first woman who would have him—a woman famed, according to my father, for her application of the "evil eye." Henry's failure, over the years, to rise through the ranks of the architectural firm slowly eroded what was left of his good nature—the small portion that hadn't been depleted by his wife. He began to experience deep and extended periods of depression, interrupted by sudden fits of rage, for which my grandmother made him profoundly sorry afterward. Through all this he continued to paint. But he could not give away his paintings, let alone sell them. They lacked that element of inspiration that elevates a work of art to greatness. Henry Doyle was not an inspired man. Eventually he took the hint. His disenchantment with his apparent lack of talent fostered a keen distaste for all things creative. He railed at his growing children if they displayed the slightest interest in the arts. "Get it through your heads," he would shout at his bewildered offspring. "The Doyles are not creative!"

One day, long after my father had graduated from business school and married Helen Chadwick, Henry Doyle's entire oeuvre was destroyed in a fire. Thanks to the quick response of the fire department, the blaze was contained within the single room, my grandfather's studio. But not before every shred of evidence that he had ever painted was incinerated. The fire was officially classified accidental, although there was plenty of unofficial speculation. A month after the studio fire incinerated his creative output, Henry Doyle died of a heart attack, so the story goes. Popular lore has it that Henry burnt his art, then took his life, a final desperate attempt to escape enduring failure, not to mention my grandmother's evil eye. But he failed even in that. My grandmother wasted no time pursuing him into the afterlife, where she could nag him for all eternity.

My father's revenge for being denied his true calling was to acquire his bachelor's degree and take it to the radio business anyway.

He has been miserably employed in the dubious industry for more than a quarter century.

He once showed me the appalling photographic evidence that he had once been a hippie—the inevitable result of an autocratic upbringing, he claims, but I chalk it up to a mere phase. The crowning achievement of his misspent youth, he has told me, was seeing Jimi Hendrix play live in a Detroit nightclub. The retelling of this story invariably causes my mother to roll her eyes—a Joni Mitchell fan to the end. By the time my parents met, my father was appropriately shorn, having abandoned tie-dye and mutton-chops for a blue suit and a shave. He was a senior at U. of T., well on his way to becoming his father.

I think he is secretly disappointed that I have not rebelled, as he had done. Perhaps one day I will dye my hair purple and pierce my nose, just for him. Apart from that unlikely event, he can rely on the monkeys to make him proud. Few of them, I predict, will amount to anything.

"You don't know how lucky you are," my father says to me, on a regular basis.

"Yes, I do."

"Have you been taking drugs?"

"Certainly not!" The denial is genuine. Perhaps there is a little of old Hank Doyle in me, after all. Among those who know me, my disapproval of mind-altering substances is legendary.

My father seems once again disappointed in me. He wants to tell me about his own experiences with drugs, back when he was a hippie, as a way of warning me away from the path of destruction. But he is too far removed from the Flower Power era to be convincing. He drives a mini-van. He looks uncomfortable in jeans. He is more concerned with the welfare of his mutual funds than with the safety of our soldiers who are fighting in Afghanistan in the futile war against terrorism. He wants to believe he is enlightened, but he is out of touch with me and my generation. As the voice of authority in our household, he can offer me nothing more than a body of rules to live by. His mid-life crisis compels him to live vicariously through me, but I shall deflect his efforts. I will convince him to buy a Porsche instead.

On the subject of drugs, Dado has much to say to his friend Raymond.

"There's a reason they call it dope."

They meet in the hallway after first period, and Raymond has just confessed to having smoked a joint. The fiend who is attempting to corrupt him is a defensive lineman named Mitch, a snaggletooth jock who will have nothing to fall back on, once his football career comes to nothing.

"It was just a joint. It's no big deal."

"That's what they all say in the beginning, but pretty soon you'll be sneaking outside between every class so you can smoke your joints, and before you know it you're skipping Social Studies to hang out with Mitch Gordon, and your career as a parking lot attendant is well under way. Enjoy your life, you dope."

"I think you're overreacting, again."

"Only a fool thinks the drugs will make him cool or strong or creative. It's an illusion. It makes you stupid and weak."

"Lots of great people were alcoholics or drug addicts. Look at Hemingway."

Dado is impressed that Raymond knows who Hemingway is. "Just imagine how much greater Hemingway might have been if his creativity hadn't been stunted by substances."

"He's been dead for a long time, and he's still famous."

"He died because the drugs and booze made him crazy. Besides, being famous is not the same thing as being great. Jack the Ripper is famous."

Raymond mulls this over. "Well, as far as serial killers go, he was pretty great, too. I mean, they haven't caught him yet, have they?"

"Now you're just being stupid. It must be the drugs." Dado must put his foot down, nip this in the bud before things get out of hand. "Listen, Ray—"

"Don't call me Ray."

"Listen, Ray-Gun, here's the deal. If you're going to continue to chisel away at your potential with drugs, you can find yourself a new best friend. You might as well get a tattoo and quit school. Any further education will be wasted on you. Go apply for that job as a cashier at the Esso station. Better yet, go home, put on some dirty old sweat pants and hang around in your room for the rest of your life. Those left-wing ninnies you call parents will be happy to support your drug habit, even if it drains all the funds from their retirement portfolio, which means that your father will have to continue to work long past the age of sixty-five. He'll have to re-mortgage the house to pay for your bail, and your failed stints at expensive rehab clinics. Of course, before it comes to that you'll probably be dead from HIV after sharing needles with Mitch Gordon, who'll turn out to be a homosexual transvestite, as well as a heroin addict."

"Okay, okay. Shut up, for Christ's sake. I get the picture."

"Good."

"Fuck, man, it was just a joint."

Dado has put out another fire. His day is only just beginning.

Second period is Math. I take my leave of Raymond outside Mr. Politis's classroom. Raymond waves over his shoulder, slouches away toward the gymnasium, where his athletic aspirations will no doubt be dashed. I watch him go, check for overt signs of intoxication. I think he will be okay.

Stu Hartman is sitting at my desk. He belongs to the jock faction, although I foresee that his expanding girth will soon make it impossible for him to run. He is outgrowing the sport. Stu thinks he is funny. He will say anything to get a laugh, especially if it's in some way insulting. Failure to laugh at Stu Hartman's repertoire can easily result in a violent nudge of encouragement.

Thanks to my success as a chameleon, he has never previously acknowledged my existence, so I am surprised to find him sitting at my desk. This break in our routine does not bode well. His desk across the room sits empty. A confrontation is inevitable.

After a moment, he spots me lurking over him, looking down on him.

"What do you want, geek?"

"You're in my seat." I keep my tone neutral, I do not want to provoke him.

"Who the fuck are you?"

"Danny Doyle. This is my seat."

Stu looks at the desk, then at me. "I don't see your name on it."

I point out my name, which I had etched into the hard wooden desktop with a ballpoint pen at the start of the year. Posterity comes in many forms. Future generations will thrill when they see my famous name scratched into their desk.

He shifts in the chair in order to peer more closely at my signature. I fear for the stability of my desk. Stu makes daily progress toward obesity. "It's my desk, now," he says, despite tangible evidence to the contrary. "Possession is nine-tenths of the law." I have noted that this phrase is a favourite among covetous teenagers. Stu laughs at his own cleverness.

"That leaves one-tenth in my favour," I say. I can play his game.

Stu narrows his porcine eyes. "How about if I pound you to within one tenth of your life?"

"Point taken."

I retreat to the other side of the classroom, where Stu's abandoned desk awaits. There are no other seats available. As I pass Mr. Politis's desk, he ignores me utterly. He gives special favour to the jocks, and the football players, in particular, for no reason that I can determine. The jocks are poor students, one and all. Not only can they not solve for x, they cannot fathom how a *letter* fits into mathematics, which they have been raised to believe relates to the addition and subtraction of *numbers*. Theoretical concepts fall beyond the scope of a jock's comprehension. Still, Mr. Politis dishes out to them passing grades for merely showing up to class and confessing that they "don't get the letter thing."

After I once broached the subject with him, tried to explain the discriminatory nature of his teaching methods, gently encouraged him to consider the adverse effect his fudging would have on the bell curve, he rejected my complaint with a curt wave of his paw and promptly failed me on the next quiz, even though I had answered all ten questions correctly. He picked on my steps to achieving the answers, which were, in his mind only, incomplete.

When I slide into the chair, the entire framework of the desk shimmies dangerously, suggesting one reason why Stu might have abandoned his usual station: it is in imminent danger of collapsing. From now on I shall be the first to arrive at Math class. I carefully arrange my books and try to sit still. That's when I hear a familiar voice whispering behind me.

"Hey, Hosanna Boyle."

I spot Frank Dolan sitting two seats back, in the next row. When our eyes meet, he snaps the rubber band between his fingers and grins. A quick glance at Stu Hartman confirms my suspicion. Stu is dabbing at his right ear, checking for blood on his fingers. He has taken my seat in order to get out of Frank's line of fire. Even the most ruthless jock knows better than to mess with Frank Dolan.

But I will not surrender to this terrorism. I turn my attention to the front, where Mr. Politis is setting up the overhead projector.

In the science class monkey chain, Mr. Politis falls somewhere in the middle. He is a small, hairy man who bears a fascinating resemblance to the macaque as he hunches over his projector. The only amusement to be had in Mr. Politis's class is his tendency to spit on the transparencies as he talks, depositing a steady spray of spittle that is magnified onto the projection screen to grotesque proportions. He abandoned his Grecian homeland before I was born, but still retains a nearly impenetrable accent that seems to cause his facial muscles no end of distress, and which leaves him largely incomprehensible.

One unfortunate result of his poorly developed enunciation is a tendency to say "axe" rather than "eks," in reference to the fabled and elusive letter that we are so often called upon to solve for in his class.

The classroom is dark, except for the projection screen, on which is displayed the intricate workings of the Quadratic Formula: *Solve x^2 + 3x − 4 = 0.* Plus a splattering of spittle.

"What is *axe?*" asks Mr. Politis.

"A sharp blade used for cutting wood," says a voice from the back of the room. It is Stu Hartman. He thinks he is funny, but the joke is both ancient and lame.

Mr. Politis presses on. "Someone tell me how we find *axe.*"

"Look in the tool shed," offers Stu.

Mr. Politis looks up from his transparency and squints through the darkness, toward the back of the room. He knows where the voice is coming from. "If you're a big expert on the Quadratic Formula, Danny Doyle, maybe you can take the rest of the class off. We can do without your disturbances."

The class shrieks with laughter.

Before I can protest my innocence, Stu Hartman offers this: "Eat me, sir."

Bedlam ensues. Mr. Politis shouts above the rabble. "Out, Danny Doyle!"

I can apply the Quadratic Formula correctly, so the class will be redundant to me. Rather than face further humiliation from Stu Hartman and Mr. Politis, I quickly gather my books and make my escape into the corridor.

A free period suits Dado's mood. He can use the time to plot his revenge on Frank Dolan. Striding with grim purpose, he makes a quick stop at his locker to deposit his books, then heads towards the side exit, where the student parking lot is located.

The student lot used to be a baseball diamond, which demonstrates where the School Board's priorities lie. There are no lines or markings on the tarmac, so the space, which might sensibly hold sixty cars, is a jumble of more than a hundred. At the far end of the lot, smoke billows from the sunroof of a lime-green Honda Civic. The ground shudders beneath Danny Doyle's feet, a signal that the sub-woofers in the Honda's modified stereo system are functioning. He doesn't hear the actual sound until he covers half the distance across the lot. It is the sort of rap music that encourages random violence and misogynistic values in today's youth. Dado has spent many hours discussing the genre with Raymond.

"The lyrics are dangerous. They encourage hatred and support anarchy."

"I don't really listen to the words."

"You may not listen to them, but you hear them. They enter your subconscious, whether you want them to or not. It's subliminal."

"I just like the beat."

"Jesus, Ray. Are you on American Bandstand?"

"On what?"

"Rap music isn't even meant for people like you, like us. It's meant for those urban children who are oppressed and underprivileged."

"I'm underprivileged. My mother won't upgrade me to Xbox. I'm still living in the last century with Nintendo."

"It's not even music. It's nothing more than a cultural phenomenon, an outcry from the underclass."

"Snoop Dogg is cool," says Raymond. "I like his videos."

Dado sighs. Sometimes he begins to lose hope. "We've talked about this before, Ray. You have to stop watching so many music videos. They're corrupting your sensibilities."

"DMX is pretty good, too."

"Listen. There hasn't been a music video with any artistic merit since Grace Jones released *Slave to the Rhythm*. It's been a downhill slide ever since."

"Who's Grace Jones?"

Dado frowns, worries about his friend.

44

I approach the thrumming car. The license plate on the rear bumper vibrates noisily. The heavy smell of pot thickens the air, causes me to breathe through my mouth. I don't like the smell. The windows are tinted, but I already know that there will be at least four occupants in the car. Gangbangers travel in posses.

When I knock on the driver's-side glass, nothing happens. I knock again. The music stops. I wait. Nothing happens. As I raise my knuckles to knock a third time, the window opens two inches. A thin, reedy voice speaks through the crack. A tenor's voice. "Yeth?"

I have just made contact with Gutterball—the most feared gangbanger at Laidlaw High. "Hello, Sylvester," I say to the crack.

There is a nervous shift inside the car, like a lot of static electricity being discharged. I have made my first mistake by using Gutterball's real name. He is Sylvester Coleman, and I have known him since the fourth grade. We met in the chess club. He was a geek, then. When he entered Laidlaw, Sylvester had to make his own choice about how he was going to fit in. While I have tried to make myself invisible to danger, he has confronted—or, perhaps more accurately, *become*—the danger. He has transmogrified from a gentle and intelligent youth into a *gangsta* with a reputation for dark, much speculated upon deeds. I don't believe most of the rumours about Gutterball. He sits behind me in choir and sings like an angel. He is all slouching attitude until he opens his throat and gives voice to those hosannas. Only when he is singing does his lisp vanish, which I believe is the reason he takes the class. I am the only student at Laidlaw who is not afraid of Gutterball.

"What the fuck you want, foo?"

I let that one pass. He owes me that for calling him Sylvester. "I want to ask a favour, Gutterball." I show my respect, use his preferred moniker.

His companions chuckle. Giving favours is not on a gangbanger's daily list of priorities.

"What the fuck you think thith ith? Fucking Thalvathion Army? Thoup kitchen clothed today. Come back nektht week."

The window rolls up. The music resumes its throbbing assault on the parking lot. I will not give up so easily. I knock on the window. No response. I knock again. Again, the music stops. Again, the window slides down two inches.

"What the fuck you want?"

I lean down into the crack, determined. "I need a gun."

There is silence inside the car. Then Gutterball speaks. "Fuck. What you need a gat for?" His posse chuckles. "Everybody wanth a fucking gat, man. What the fuck?" His overuse of the word "fuck" is designed to distract others from his speech impediment.

I am not daunted. "I want to kill someone," I say, evenly. If I lie to him, he will not take me seriously and I will not get what I'm after. I know that he won't snitch on me, provided, of course, that I do not intend to kill him, or anyone in his posse.

There is another static discharge inside the car as four bodies shift in their seats. The window slides fully open and I can now see the boys inside the car. The smell of marijuana wafts out and I take the brunt of it.

Gutterball looks up at me with red eyes. "Foo, what the fuck you wan do that for?" He slouches down in his chair and looks out the windshield, as if he isn't all that interested in my answer.

"Do I have to give you a reason before you'll give me a gun?"

"Give? Man, you got the fucking Thally Anne thing goin. Nobody gonna give you nothin."

"I'll pay for it, of course. Unless I could just borrow one for the day. I'd give it back, first thing in the morning."

"Fuck. You be in jail firtht thing in the morning. You don't know thit about thmoking no one. Firtht thing in the morning you be dead. Thit, man. You thome thorry-ath-ed thucker."

"How much does a gun cost?"

"Man, you got to leave the dirty work to the profethional, fuck. You jutht thoot your own jimmy off." His boys chuckle at that.

I must talk straight and display no fear if I am to get anywhere with him. "Look, I'm trying to be serious, here. I've got money, and I want to buy a gun. Or borrow one, if I can. Either you can help me or you can't. Just tell me which it's going to be."

"What the fuck you think, foo? We just four upthanding thitithenth. We don't got no gat, man. We the fucking Boy Thcouth of America."

"Okay," I say. "Forget it." I turn to go.

"What the fuck? Hold up there, man. I just zipping you up. Thit."

I return to the window. "I can have a gun?"

"Fuck, no, man. It don't work like that. Thith ain't no fucking drive-thru gat thop. Thit."

"Maybe you can do it for me," I say. I concede that I'd rather leave the dirty work to a professional.

"What the fuck you thaying? You want me cap thome mother?"

"I'd pay you, naturally."

"Man, I mutht be trippin, you making me out thome kind of killer, thomthing. Who the fuck you want capped?"

"I can't tell you that unless you agree to do it."

"No, man. Fuck that. You thome trippin fucker. Thit." The window slides up. The music resumes.

I am alone.

Dado is not discouraged. He goes to the library, where he can sit quietly for the remainder of second period. He absently leafs through a copy of *Schizophrenia Revealed: From Neurons to Social Interactions*, a new acquisition for the school. He will discreetly remove it from the library, for the good of all.

He feels strange, wonders if perhaps he has inhaled too much second-hand smoke in the parking lot. He has trouble concentrating. He sits in a study booth, where three low walls protect him from the few roaming students who have second period off, and also from the watchful gaze of the chief librarian, a humourless dowager with a manifest distaste for children. He sets his head down on the table and shuts his eyes.

Frank Dolan's face wavers, insubstantial, yet as large as the known universe, a menacing, hideous black hole that sucks in everything that is good. Dado is slowly, inexorably drawn into the vortex. From the infinite depths of nothingness comes a voice.

You're a chicken shit, Boyle.

I'm a chameleon.

You are prey and I am predator.

I pray for your death.

God cannot help you. I cannot die, you fool.

I'm invisible. You can't hurt me if you can't see me.

I see everything, Boyle. Even with my eyes closed I can see you.

You see nothing.

You are nothing. That's what I see.

I'll kill you.

I hear the hosannas, but they aren't for me.

You have no reason to hate me.

I have no reason to like you.

I don't understand your hatred.

You understand shit, Boyle. You cannot begin to comprehend my power. You can solve for x, but I am not x.

You are the devil.

The devil answers to me.

You will answer to me, I promise you that.

Your feeble threats bore me, Boyle. Go ahead and get your gun, little man. I am bullet-proof.

Dado knows the truth of it, and it makes him feel helpless. He is a beetle in a jar. The scope of his universe has been reduced to an empty Miracle Whip jar with a hole nailed into the tin lid that offers just enough air to survive. Unseen eyes peer at him through the glass walls. Thick fingers manipulate the jar, shake it, turn it upside down, prepare to smash it once the fun is gone. The beetle rolls around inside, powerless.

I am throwing grains of sand at the elephant. I am not crazy.

Chapter 5

The voice in my dream is not Frank Dolan, although it is a convincing impersonation. I am impressed, but not fooled. Frank is merely a boy who does not know how to make friends. The voice has been around longer than Frank has; it has been around longer than I. The voice remembers the birth of big-G God as if it were yesterday. And it laughs. I know that God doesn't exist because the voice does exist.

I have asked the voice what its name is, but it scoffs.

You cannot name me, Boyle. I am unnamable.

"How can I worship you, if I can't name you?" I have periodic bouts of sarcasm.

I don't expect you to worship me. I expect you to fear me.

I have given the voice a name, anyway. I call it Dog. Big *D*.

Dog first spoke to me when I was five. It asked me if it wouldn't be fun to hit my brother Lem. I said yes, of course. What five-year-old doesn't like hitting his younger brother? Lem responded as always by crying. Of all my siblings, he is the one who clings the most to that unseemly aspect of early childhood; Lem was, and remains, a crybaby. Still, until Dog spoke to me, I had been happily amusing myself on the other side of the room with some plastic soldiers. I had barely registered Lem's presence in the room until Dog made his playful suggestion.

My mother eventually responded to Lem's pitiful yelps. She pulled me off him and gave my bottom a good slapping, and then quickly skittled off to resume her household duties. She had a demanding infant and a growing foetus to contend with, my poor mother.

Later that day I found her in the kitchen. "Mommy?"

"Hm?" She was cooking.

"Someone talked to me."

"That's nice, hon."

"Not a real person. It was in my head."

"You have a wonderful imagination, Daniel."

"Imagination is pretend, right?"

"Uh-huh."

"It was a voice. It talked to me."

"You were just thinking."

"What's that?"

She had to stop stirring, in order to concentrate on her answer. "We all have a voice in our heads. It's our own voice and it talks to us. We call it thinking."

I considered that theory. "Do you have a voice?"

"Yes, hon."

"And it talks to you?"

"Sure, hon."

"What does it say?"

She had to stop stirring again. "Oh, I don't know. Sometimes it reminds me to pick up margarine when I'm out, later. Sometimes it tells me I'm tired, and should go to bed. Things like that."

"My voice didn't sound like me. It told me to hit Lem."

My mother gave me a stern sideways glance, then her face softened. "Well, you're a boy. That's the sort of thing boys your age think about, I've discovered."

"I didn't want to do it."

"Well, next time don't listen to the voice."

"Okay."

"Unless it tells you to clean up your room."

During a moment of weakness, I attempted to raise the subject, as a theory, with Raymond.

"Do you ever hear voices," I asked, "you know, in your head?"

"You mean like ghosts?"

"Sure."

He thought for a moment. "Well..."

"Yes?"

"The other day I thought my dead Uncle Morris was calling me, but it turned out to be gas."

"Don't make jokes, Ray. I'm serious." I punched him in the arm.

50

"Jeez. Don't call me Ray."

I punched him in the arm again, because that is part of the bonding ritual between young men. "Just answer the question properly, stupid."

Raymond took a moment to choose his words carefully. "Nope."

"Never?"

"Well, when I was a kid I pretended I had an imaginary friend."

"That doesn't make sense. An imaginary friend *is* pretend. How can you *pretend* to have one?"

"I heard my parents talking about it, one day. They were saying how some study showed that children with imaginary friends were more likely to be gifted, so I asked them what 'gifted' meant. I thought about what they said, and decided I wanted them to think I was gifted. So I made up an imaginary friend. His name was Bob."

"Bob? Jesus Christ. You have no imagination whatsoever. Couldn't you think of something more original than Bob?"

He shrugged. "They bought it. That's all that matters."

"Unbelievable. Your parents never cease to amaze me."

"They were always asking me what Bob and I talked about, or what we did today, or whatever, and I'd make up a lot of shit. After a few years Bob just sort of faded away and my parents stopped asking about him."

"Naturally."

"Of course, I never told them about my secret audience."

"Your what?"

"I have a secret audience that watches me all the time."

"Watches you?"

"When I'm doing stuff, playing dodge-ball or riding my bike, or whatever, they watch me."

"They just watch?"

"Sometimes they applaud."

"Applaud—"

"When I used to play pee-wee hockey, they were my cheering section."

"Weren't there real people in the stands to do that?"

"Sure, but they weren't all cheering just for me."

"And this audience follows you around all day, watching everything you do?"

"Yep. I don't let them in the bathroom, though. A man needs

some privacy."

"So, right now we have an invisible audience watching us?"

"They're not invisible. *That* would be crazy. I can see them in my mind."

"What do they look like?"

"Just people. I can't really see their faces. They're sitting in bleachers, but it's sort of dark. Do you think that makes me crazy?"

"Ray, you're the sanest person I know. Can you tell if they have antennae? Or a third eye?"

He looked at me warily and determined the question was rhetorical. "You don't have to make fun of me. You're the one who asked."

Danny Doyle lifts his head from the table in the study cubicle. He is alone. He is sweating. The bell has rung, signalling the end of period two. He has not solved his problem, but an embryonic plan is formulating in his mind. He wonders if Dog has planted the seed, and dismisses the question as irrelevant. One way or another he will deal with Frank Dolan.

He abandons the psychology textbook in the study cubicle. Dado feels reckless today. He will steal it some other time.

Third period is Social Studies. He likes the class, and he likes the teacher, Ms. Wilcox. He likes the ambiguity of *Ms.* He does not know if Ms. Wilcox is married or not, and he isn't interested in finding out, but he enjoys the mystery of the title. Ms. Wilcox's age is as indeterminate as her marital status. She could be twenty-eight or forty-eight. She is a trim and neat woman of similarly indeterminate beauty, whose general attractiveness can be credited in part to her not having acquired the grim indolence of her academic peers. The atmosphere in her classroom is tranquil and positive. And she considers Danny Doyle among her favourites.

Danny is the first to arrive. He does not want to take any chances with the seating arrangements. He takes his place in the rear and calmly awaits the second bell. Ms. Wilcox smiles at him from her station at the front, and Danny briefly wonders what she looks like naked; her clothes give away nothing. He has never seen a naked woman, other than through the miracle of photography and, of course, classical art. He shakes off the thought when he realizes how inappropriate it is.

Marion Dalton is the last to arrive as the second bell sounds. She glides to her seat near the front and makes an egregious effort to avoid eye contact with Danny.

"Okay, class," says Ms. Wilcox. "Last time we were discussing moral justification for the Crusades. I think we can all agree that no agreement can really be had on this topic. Who can tell me why?"

No hands go up.

"Marion?"

Ms. Wilcox has a sly sense of humour. She knows that any subject that doesn't relate to shopping will be lost on Marion.

"Um—"

"Anyone?"

No one else volunteers, so I must. My hand rises.

"Yes, Danny?"

"The issue at stake is faith, which is the single most volatile issue between men. The catalyst for just about every major conflict in history can be traced back to faith."

"But surely wars are fought for many reasons. Tiffs between neighbouring Kings, desire for riches and battlefield glory. The Trojan War was fought over a woman."

"The great love between Helen and Paris is a wonderful fiction, but would have had little to do with Agamemnon's beef with the Trojans. Back then, every war was fought for, or in collusion with, the gods. When Alaric led the Visigoth army over the hills into Rome, he may have told his people that he was fighting for their freedom, or maybe he thought he was paying too much for an amphora of good Falernian wine and decided to cut out the middleman, but what he was really after was glory in the eyes of his gods. His own faith couldn't permit him to tolerate all those Christians roaming the known world, spreading their blasphemy to the peasants and contradicting his own beliefs. To permit that is to show weakness in your faith, and a leader in particular must set the benchmark for faith if he is to survive. Ask yourself why Europeans colonized so much of Africa? Real estate? Power? A stronger tax base? The prospect of gold? Those things were secondary. They were the gravy. The real aim was to rid the world of pagan superstition. And because they believed so strongly in God, they were able to believe they were doing the right thing by occupying those native lands. They were saving souls. They were doing the Lord's work. They were so bamboozled by faith, they couldn't see that they were annihilating scores of the most ancient cultures on Earth. They effectively trampled a living history out of existence. The loss to anthropology is immeasurable. More recently, even Hitler believed he had God on his side, which goes to show you that even crackpots and tyrants are driven by faith." I regret that Raymond is not here to hear this.

Dado stays up each night to watch the late news with his father. They sit at opposite ends of the sofa and silently witness the decline of civilization on a twenty-six-inch flickering screen. It is a bonding experience for both men.

I have faith in no gods, but I hold in fervent esteem Ms. Wilcox's teaching method, which is to act as mediator, rather than pedagogue. She does not dictate facts, nor does she assign reading material to be memorized, and then regurgitated in an exam. She gently pricks us with simple questions that force us—some of us—to formulate our own ideas about our world and its people. At Laidlaw she is uniquely effective.

"Very good, Danny. Let's look more closely at the colonization of Africa. Wouldn't it be safe to say that Europeans, especially those who were setting out to pioneer the New World, were simply mining Africa for slaves? After all, someone had to do the dirty work in the American colonies and the Europeans certainly weren't going to do it themselves, were they?"

I hold my tongue, permitting my colleagues the opportunity to participate. I have noted how they rely on me to carry the burden in Social Studies, and I'm aware that I do them no favour by dominating the discussion. They must have their turn, if they are to learn anything.

Hesty Goldberg rises to the challenge. "I think they, like, shouldn't have brought the blacks over here." My classmates are, for the most part, like Hesty: inarticulate boobs. But I give Hesty partial marks for making an effort.

"Why?" asks Ms. Wilcox. "Don't you like black people?"

Twenty-four pairs of eyes shift toward Gutterball's empty chair. I know where he is.

"God, no! I mean, yes!"

From my vantage at the back I can see the beads of sweat leaping off poor Hesty's brow.

"I didn't mean it like that. I mean, like, I just think it was wrong. They should have left the slaves where they were."

"So, you're saying they should have kept the slaves in Africa?"

"Sure. I mean, that's where they belong. Well…that's, like, their home—"

I can bear no more. My hand goes up. "The native African was a victim of faith. Or, more accurately, of prejudice, which is an unfortunate by-product of faith. It was prejudice against the African's strange and incomprehensible belief system that compelled the European to take action. The African was deemed primitive because he carved idols out of stone and tramped around the countryside buck-naked. Never mind that it was a hundred degrees in the shade. Everything was measured against the standards of polite European society, which was both unfair and short-sighted. Anyway, the African was regarded as unsophisticated, and therefore inferior in all other ways, including intelligence. And that prejudice has stuck to this day. On the other hand, the missionaries must have paid at least a small price in sweat, toiling in the steaming jungles for God in their black robes."

Ms. Wilcox nods. "We've abolished slavery. Are we not enlightened?"

"Slavery still exists," I say. "It's just cleverly disguised as oppression. The tradition of slavery goes back much further than the colonization of Africa. The Romans collected slaves as booty. Most of them weren't black, although a Nubian might fetch a higher price at the local slave market, just for the exotic factor. Mostly they were Persians or Gauls. The Gauls were also considered boorish and unsophisticated, with their wild red hair and guttural speech. It wasn't uncommon for a careless Gallic prince to find himself serving honeyed dates to a senator's daughter on the Esquiline."

As always, I have impressed Ms. Wilcox with my lucid ideas and attention to detail. I rightly earn my A+.

"All right, then," says Ms. Wilcox. "Who can tell me…"

I tune her out. I've made my contribution to the lesson. I feel tired and slightly nauseated, a residual effect of Gutterball's parking lot reefer. I lean my head against the back wall and shut my eyes.

You are prey and I am predator.

I am a chameleon.

Dado's eyes open. The classroom is at the end of a long, dark tunnel. There are faraway voices, Ms. Wilcox, and other anonymous voices, animal sounds; inhuman sounds. Raymond is suddenly standing in the tunnel, eyes round, two perfect Os, mouth another perfect O, a siren of fear, a wail of helplessness. *Help me...help me,* arms orbiting, swatting non-existent flies. *Please...help me.* Dado is made of stone, cannot move. Raymond turns to run, is pursued by a sound, a darkness, a monumental wisp of tangible nothingness, blackness growing, swallowing Raymond, consuming everything.

He is prey.

The tunnel opens on Raymond's face.

"C'mon, man. Let's go. I'm starving."

Danny is in the hallway, his books under his arm. He doesn't remember leaving Ms. Wilcox's classroom.

Raymond squints. "You all right? Your eyes are red."

Danny is not sure if he can move. With some effort, he slowly turns his head to the left, and then to the right. "I'm okay," he says. "Just a stiff neck."

"What were you saying to Marion Dalton?"

"Marion?"

"Just now. What did you say to her?"

"Nothing. What would I ever want to say to Marion?"

"I don't know, man. I saw you talking to her when I was coming down the hall."

"You're seeing things. I wasn't talking to her."

"It looked like you were whispering something in her ear. Shit. You don't have to tell me if you don't want. I was just asking. It's not like I'm jealous."

Danny is confused. "Whatever it was, it couldn't have been important."

Raymond looks peeved. "Forget it, man. I don't care. With these zits, she won't look at me, anyway." He gives Danny a light shove in the direction of the cafeteria. "Let's go. I want to get a good seat."

"I'll catch up. I need to stop at my locker."

Raymond trots away and Danny engages his purposeful stride in the opposite direction. His locker is at the end of the row, near the east exit. He is jostled by fifteen-hundred students who leave the premises during the lunch hour. As he drops his books onto the locker shelf, he detects a presence behind him, and a shiver willows up his spine.

He turns around.

"Hi, Danny. I thought about what you said." Marion Dalton leans in and kisses him.

Chapter 6

Marion Dalton is sensationally blonde. Light radiates from her in an otherworldly fashion. It is nearly impossible to avoid staring at her because she is a flawless example of human engineering. In the hallways, necks crane and heads swivel as she passes. At the beginning of each semester, when the student body assembles in the gymnasium to suffer another tedious speech from our principal, it is Marion Dalton who is the focus of two thousand adoring eyes. Even the girls of Laidlaw cannot resist looking at her. They study her, scrutinize her, break down her components in order to understand better what they are lacking. For every teenager, Marion represents the acme of adolescent desire: blinding beauty that commands total attention, total devotion, total submission.

One of the most predictable truths in life is the correlation between beautiful women and the rumour mill. The sniff of scandal forever shrouds Marion.

It was rumoured, for instance, that Marion was having a secret affair with Mr. Cunningham, the physics teacher, throughout the tenth grade—an accusation that has never been proven, but persists with the vigour of the most preposterous lies. I deemed it unlikely because Mr. Cunningham is, from my perspective, so very old, and not the least attractive. After that came whispers that Marion was seen about town with another older man, apparently a creative director at an advertising agency. That one I believed.

The most recent scandal resulted in a police investigation after a nude photo of Marion appeared on an adult website. Raymond and I conducted a private investigation into the matter using his home computer, and saw the offending evidence with our own eyes. Whoever perpetrated this act needs a lighter touch with the

Photoshop airbrush. The body beneath Marion's head clearly belonged to another woman—a redhead from whom the corporeal gloss of adolescence had long ago fled. The case is still open, although the pornographic image has been removed from the website—not before every boy at Laidlaw, except yours truly, downloaded it to his hard drive.

I am forced to rely on my friend's technology when I need to make contact with the outside world. The Doyle household remains one of the last holdouts against modernization. My mother is implacable in her misguided belief that the Doyles do not need a computer.

"It's a necessary tool for research," I say.

"If you look on the shelves in the living room you'll find an entire volume of Encyclopedia Britannica. They're called books, and they served your father and me perfectly well, over the years."

"Those books are so old, they still claim the Earth is flat. They predict that one day man will fly to the moon."

"I'm not going to shell out a thousand dollars just to make it easy for you to find pictures of naked women." My mother knows what goes on out there on the Information Highway.

"I don't need a computer to get porn. I can find all the naked women I want in the garage, in Dad's secret stash of Penthouse." The disclosure of my father's antiquated collection of smut may not go over well with the rest of the monkeys—or with my father, for that matter—but it's for their ultimate good if I can sway my mother's opinion. "If you want your sons to get well-paying jobs, they'll need computer skills in order to compete in a progressive job market."

"We've gotten along without it for this long. You are all smart boys. You'll have no trouble getting jobs."

"That's just the sort of twentieth-century thinking that's holding us back. You need to grow with the times. You need to adapt. It's a fundamental principle of evolution."

"I've evolved quite enough, thank you. Save up your money and buy your own computer, if you feel so strongly about it."

"I shouldn't have to do that. That's precisely my point. All the other kids have computers at home."

"I should warn you, Daniel, that after raising six boys, I'm allergic to any sentence that begins with 'All the other kids…'"

"You'll be sorry in a few years when you're serving Sunday dinner to five squeegee kids and a forklift driver." Even though I have unlimited access to Raymond's computer, I must make my argument, on principle. Besides, I might like a copy of Marion Dalton's ersatz body for my own private scrutiny.

Back to Marion: One person who has energetically endeavoured to quash the ever-evolving catalogue of rumours is Marion's ex-boyfriend, Vick Peterman. It took less than a week for Vick and Marion to begin dating after they arrived at Laidlaw. The beautiful people have a way of finding each other in the crowd. But their relationship ended suddenly over the past Christmas holidays, after more than two years, and the gossip surrounding the split has been as entertaining and prolific as the Hollywood tabloids. One story has it that Vick discovered the truth of the Cunningham rumour and walked out in a jealous rage, threatening to kill both Marion and the physics teacher. The other camp claimed it was Vick who was caught cheating, not only with another girl but with Nicole Welt, Marion's best friend and co-captain of the cheerleading squad. Another version had Marion transmit to Vick an unnamed venereal disease. And there were variations on the theme of physical abuse, regularly doled out by the star athlete.

Regardless of what else may or may not be true, I believe the part about Vick's abusive behaviour. He has a mean streak that must make Frank Dolan blush with envy. As the kingpin of the jock faction, Vick is a creative leader in the art of torturing the geeks of Laidlaw. The only thing I will put in his favour is that he has ignored me for all these years. I fear that is about to change.

I back out of Marion's kiss, back into my locker door, my lips burning with fear. I can taste Marion's candy-flavoured lipstick. "What are you doing?"

Her eyes turn to glass. For the first time, she seems vulnerable to me. "Thanking you."

"For what?" I have never had a blackout before. It makes me nervous that I have done things that I can't remember.

"For what you said."

"What did I say?"

"You know."

"I'd appreciate it if you'd remind me."

"Don't spoil a special moment by joking, Danny."

"If you knew anything about me, you'd know that I never joke."

Dog has done this to me. I know he is responsible. I am helpless to defend myself against him. I am helpless to defend myself against Marion Dalton.

She glides forward and kisses me again. I have nowhere to go, I am trapped, I am torn in many directions. I haven't asked for this, but it's not unpleasant. However, nothing Marion Dalton does goes unnoticed. Many people have just witnessed our exchange of saliva, and soon Vick Peterman will know about it, too. He will not be happy. He has had trouble letting go of his feelings for Marion, even though they have not been together for more than a month.

Marion releases me from her grip and clips away, toward the cafeteria. "See you later, Danny," she says, waving a manicured hand over her shoulder as if we were the oldest of friends.

I am speechless.

I look to my left and spot Heidi Borland, who stands ten strides away, clutching her books to her chest. She looks appalled.

Dado makes a monumental decision: it is time to end the game, come clean, open himself completely to Heidi Borland, or lose her forever. He must explain the misleading scene she has just witnessed. He must confess his devotion to her, and demand reciprocation. The time for games is done.

He closes his locker and approaches Heidi.

When she detects my intention, she begins to move toward the lunchroom. She does not want a confrontation, but she must pass me if she wants to get to the cafeteria.

I reach for her arm. "Wait. I want to talk to you."

She pulls in her arm at the last second, dodges around me neatly.

I follow. "Wait a minute, Heidi. Please."

The back of her head says everything she wants to say.

"Let me explain," I plead.

Heidi suddenly stops, nearly causing a rear-end collision. She turns. "Explain what?" To her, the game goes on.

"What you saw, back there. It was a misunderstanding."

"What do you think I saw, Danny?"

"You know what you saw. Marion Dalton kissing me."

"Good for you."

"Quite the contrary, I assure you."

"You don't need to assure me of anything. What you do with Marion Dalton, or anyone else, is entirely your business."

"Setting aside the fact that any minute now Vick Peterman is going to fold me up and stuff me down a sewer grate, are you telling me you have no reaction to my being kissed by Marion?"

She shrugs. "I wouldn't have pegged her as your type, since you asked."

"Who do you think is my type?"

She shrugs again. "Someone smarter than Marion, I suppose."

"You're smarter than Marion."

"A gerbil is smarter than Marion."

"True. Nevertheless, I think you're avoiding the point."

"What is the point?"

"The point is us."

"That's pretty poor grammar for someone so smart."

"I don't want to play the game anymore, Heidi."

"What game?"

"This game."

"Is this a game?"

"Yes. I don't want to play it."

"Okay."

She turns to go, and I grab her. "Wait." I lighten my grip, but do not let go. "Listen."

"I'm listening."

"I'm going to ask you a question and I'd like you to answer it truthfully."

"Okay."

I let go of her. I feel my forehead getting hot, feel that my inexperience with girls is exposing me. "Do you like me?"

"I have no reason not to like you."

"That's a vague answer."

"Your question was vague. I like a lot of things. I like thunderstorms and white chocolate. I like William Shakespeare. I like Mrs. Banks and my cat, Mitzi. I dislike a lot of things, too. Some things I have no opinion of at all."

"Are you saying you have no opinion of me?"

"No."

"What are you saying, then?"

"What are you asking?"

"You're still playing the game."

"I like games."

"I like games, too, but I'm tired of this one. I just want to have a normal conversation with you."

"I don't know if that's possible. You're not a normal person."

I bristle at this. "What does that mean?"

"I think it's unlikely anyone can have a normal conversation with you."

"Are you saying I'm abnormal? Because I happen to know something about the subject."

"I fear you know something about a lot of subjects."

"What about the subject of us?"

"So, we're back on that, are we?"

"It's a pressing subject."

"What's the rush?"

"I want to know if you like me. You know exactly what I mean, so give me a proper answer."

"Okay."

"Is that your answer?"

"No."

"What is your answer?"

"Yes."

"Is that your answer?"

"Yes."

"You like me?"

"Yes."

"I like you, too."

"I didn't ask."

"Nevertheless."

She doesn't look like someone who likes me. She looks like someone who is angry with me. Or worse: disappointed.

"Is there something bothering you?"

"That's another potentially vague question, Danny."

"There's nothing going on between Marion and me."

"Marion might disagree."

"She was just thanking me for something I said to her."

"Whatever you said must have been quite good."

"I wish I knew. The point is, there's nothing between us."

"So you've said. It has nothing to do with me."

"But you just admitted you like me."

"I did."

"And I admitted I like you."

"You did."

"Don't you see a bigger meaning to that?"

"Do you have something else you want to ask me?"

I cannot hesitate or the moment will be lost. "Do you want to go out with me sometime?"

"You mean like a date?"

"Yes."

"No."

"Why not?"

"You ask too many questions."

"Is that your reason?"

"See what I mean? There you go again with the questions."

"Is it?"

"No. It's just an observation."

"We'd make a good couple."

"You're thinking somewhat beyond a first date."

"I'm a forward thinker."

"Do you see us married, living in a house somewhere, raising children?"

"I haven't thought that far ahead, no."

"Do you see us sleeping together?"

"Yes."

"I find that hard to believe, after what I just saw between you and Marion Dalton."

"I thought we'd already settled that issue. Let's not talk about her anymore."

"What do you want to talk about, then?"

"How about your reason for not going out with me? Are you seeing someone else?"

"I prefer older men."

"You're being evasive."

"I'm aware of that."

"Anyway, I'm not that young. I'll be eighteen in a few months."

"Time's running out."

"What do you mean?"

"To make the deadline. Doesn't every boy at Laidlaw want to

have sex before his eighteenth birthday?"

"Who told you that?" She didn't answer. "Anyway, what makes you think I'm still a virgin?"

She looks at me as if the answer were written on my face. "Are you?"

"That's a pretty personal question from someone who won't go out with me. What if I were to ask you that question?"

"Go ahead."

"Are you a virgin?"

"You answer me first."

"Yes."

"Is that your answer?"

"Yes. Your turn."

"I can't tell you."

"Why not? I just told you my answer."

"Boys have nothing to lose by answering that question."

"You have nothing to lose, either."

"Yes, I do. Respect."

"That's nonsense. I have complete respect for you."

"If I say no, you'll think less of me. You'll demand to know who I've been with, and when, and how many times. You'll think I'm a slut."

"I will not."

"You may not say it, but you'll think it. If I say yes, you'll think I'm a prude."

"I will not."

"You'll think it."

"I think you underestimate me."

"I think I have you sized up."

"I think you're really great." I have once again used a weak adjective and a lame adverb. For some reason Heidi causes me to fluster. I must be in love. "Nothing you tell me about yourself can change that."

"I believe that's true," she says. "It's called infatuation, and it makes boys more stupid than usual."

"I'm not infatuated with you. I'm—"

"Shut up! Don't you dare say those words to me."

"How do you know what I'm going to say?"

"You don't know me well enough to be in love with me."

"That can be rectified if you go out with me."

"Honestly, Danny. Maybe you're not as smart as I thought. Dating is a reciprocal thing. If I'm going to go out with you, I have to be interested in knowing you better, too. It's not all about what you want."

"I want you to know more about me. I know what dating is all about."

"When was your last date?"

"That's another personal question from someone who won't go out with me."

"We're starting to talk in circles," she says. "I'm going to go eat my lunch now."

"Will you eat lunch with me?"

"I don't think so. I'd just be encouraging you, and that wouldn't be fair."

"Can we at least be friends?"

"That will never satisfy you. If we try to be friends, you won't be able to look at me without thinking about me sexually."

"You think I can't be just friends with a girl?"

"I think you can't be just friends with me. You appear to have failed at being just friends with Marion. You have a track record."

"Marion Dalton doesn't interest me. Let's not talk about her anymore."

"Let's not talk anymore, period." She turns and leaves me standing alone in the corridor. I watch her round the corner.

That didn't turn out the way I expected.

I find Raymond at our usual table in the cafeteria, on the perimeter. From that vantage, we have a panoramic view of the vast chamber. The cafeteria reverberates with teenage shrieks and mindless chatter.

"I heard about you and Marion," he says, as I sit. News travels fast at Laidlaw. "Way to go, man. If you weren't my friend, I'd have to hate you."

"It was just a little misunderstanding. Nothing to worry about."

"Who's worrying? I just want to know what your secret is."

"Unless you can tell me what I said to Marion outside Ms. Wilcox's class, I'm afraid the mystery will endure."

"You're a little weird today. You okay?"

"I'm not feeling quite myself, to be honest."

I spot Heidi at her usual table at the far end of the room. As always, she sits in silence with her shifty gang, and makes a point of not looking my way. She is eating an apple, which is not enough food to sustain a teenager's active lifestyle. She should be having fries soaked in thick gravy if she wants to make it through the afternoon. I resist the temptation to advise her.

"Where's your lunch," Raymond asks.

"I'm not hungry." The nutritious lunch, lovingly prepared by my mother, remains in my locker. I cannot be seen with a paper-bag lunch.

I spy Marion Dalton. She radiates light from her usual throne in the center of the room, where everyone can see her. I have noticed that the seniors prefer to take the same place each day in the cafeteria. It is the first sign that they are about to step into an adult world: this need for routine. The juniors and sophomores move around, try out different tables. They are still searching to find their place in life.

"There's too much gravy on these fries," I say, licking my fingers.

Raymond looks down at his quickly-disappearing fries, then gives me a hard look. "I thought you weren't hungry?"

I ignore his rebuke, help myself to his greasy platter. I want to tell him about my confrontation with Heidi Borland, but I would then be forced to admit that she won't go out with me, and I must not appear to fail in my friend's eyes. Sooner or later Heidi will come to me. "Have you seen Vick?" Vick's routine has been upset by his breakup with Marion. He is no longer welcome at the center table.

Raymond speaks with a mouth full of dripping fries. "He left right after Marion showed up. He seemed pretty mad."

"I'm going to have to take the long way home, after school."

"What else is new?" says Raymond.

Frank Dolan does not know everything about Dado. He does not know, for instance, that Dado has a secret escape route from school property. Dado must break rules in order to effect the escape, but at times rules must be broken. He is resigned.

Danny picks at Raymond's fries until there is only a messy brown sludge remaining on the plate.

"Would you like anything else for lunch, sir?" asks Raymond, obsequiously. I am not the only one with a sarcastic streak.

"No. I'm not hungry."

"Marion keeps looking over at you."

I bring her into focus, and indeed she favours me with a faint smile that four hundred others witness. I spot several jocks trotting out of the cafeteria, no doubt in search of their leader, bursting with an update on my lurid involvement with his ex-girlfriend. I am no longer safe in the lunchroom.

"Let's get out of here."

Partway across the room, I force Raymond to go back and pick up his tray.

"They pay someone to do that," he protests.

He is referring to Tray Lady, an ancient, arthritic woman with a hunched back and inoperable cataracts. She is too old to work. She should be knitting afghans in a nursing home, not schlepping dirty trays after thoughtless adolescents.

"Shame on you, Ray. How will you feel when Tray Lady has a stroke, thanks to your laziness?"

He knows I will not let the subject drop. "Jesus, man. It's just a tray." He goes back for it.

"One good deed each day," I remind him, "can outweigh ten bad ones." I am full of useful aphorisms.

My success at Laidlaw as a chameleon is facilitated in part by maintaining several good hiding places within the building. We adjourn to my favourite lunchtime hideout: the dark and isolated crawlspace beneath the stage. The stage is located at the south end of the gymnasium, so our low voices are lost beneath the clamour of the girls' basketball team, which practices over the lunch hour on Tuesdays and Thursdays. The clap of the basketball, the squeak of sneakers, the terse shouts of open players: "Here! Over here!", the coach's shrill whistle, all combine to offer us cover. Entry to the crawlspace is beyond two unmarked and windowless doors. I discovered early on that the Laidlaw corridors are smattered with a number of these anonymous doors. Presumably, the lack of markings makes these doors less of an enticement to curious students than a sign that explicitly forbids entry.

We settle on a soft pile of wrestling mats.

"You should bring Marion here," says Raymond, stretching out on his back. "You could have some fun on these mats."

"It would really help if you'd try to understand that I want

68

nothing to do with Marion, on these mats or anywhere else."

"Did she give you tongue?"

"Don't be crass." I remember the kiss and soften a bit. "It was a pretty good kiss."

"Hm."

"Not that I'm any kind of expert."

"She's something, all right. I'd give anything to spend an hour in here with her."

But I can think only of Heidi. Raymond and I spend a few minutes consumed by our respective fantasies. My own thoughts are soon intruded upon by the spectre of Frank Dolan. He must spoil everything.

"Does your father own a gun?" I ask, breaking the silence.

"Not that I know of. Why?"

"I was just wondering."

"Bullshit. You're up to something."

"You're pretty suspicious, Ray. What makes you think I'm not going to talk to you about firearm safety in the household? Do you know how many kids die each year thanks to carelessly stored guns in the home?"

"Don't be an asshole. What are you up to? Does it have something to do with Frank?"

"It's better if I don't talk about it. It's for your own protection."

"You're going to shoot Frank?"

I refuse to answer.

Raymond reads my mind. "You're nuts. You want to go to jail for the rest of your life over a jerk like him?"

"First of all, I'm still a juvenile. I'd be out of the slammer in three months. This is my last chance to do something about him before the Young Offender's Act no longer applies to me. Second of all, everything has a price. I just have to figure out whether or not the price is worth it."

"You've said yourself that Frank's just lonely. Why don't you try and talk to him? Be his friend. Jesus. If you want to kill someone, it should be Vick Peterman. There'd be a lot of grateful geeks if you did."

"Let the geeks do their own dirty work."

"Even if you had a gun, you'd never be able to use it. You'd chicken out at the last minute, and then Frank would take the gun away and shoot *you.*"

"I could do it. I know I could do it."

"Anyway, the only place you'd get a gun around here is from Gutterball."

"I tried him."

"Shit. You're serious."

"Of course I'm serious. When have you ever known me not to be serious?"

"You're starting to scare me, man."

"I told you I didn't want to talk about it, but now you're involved. You have to help me."

"I'm not helping you. You're nuts."

"You're my best friend. You have to help, those are the rules."

"You've been so weird, lately, it's hard to tell when you're serious."

"I'm always serious." I give Raymond a brief pause to reflect on the importance of loyalty among friends.

"Anyway, you should just forget about the gun. That's a stupid idea."

"Let's hear your brilliant plan, Einstein."

He takes a few moments to devise a brilliant plan. "Think of a way to scare the hell out of him, maybe even hurt him a little."

"A little?"

"Hurt him so he knows you're serious, but scare him a lot, so he leaves you alone. Make him think you're going to kill him, make him shit his pants, then let him go. He won't bother you again."

I ponder his suggestion. "That's a perfectly reasonable plan, Ray, but Frank must die." Perhaps I can do it without a gun, after all. Perhaps I will borrow elements from Raymond's plan, but the result must be final.

Chapter 7

Dado has a plan.

In Danny Doyle's household, his mother makes the plans. She holds a bachelor's degree in planning and wields it like a truncheon. The rest of the Doyles are resigned.

Helen Doyle (nee Chadwick) was the bossy eldest of four girls born not more than a year apart. Three of the girls grew into local beauties in their hometown of Fenlon Falls. Only the youngest, Joy, suffered tangibly for her love of food. She has grappled with her weight for most of her life.

Once the girls grew beyond the age when they could be spanked, Ralston Chadwick's paternal role in the estrogen-rich home was reduced to silent provider. By the time Helen was a teenager, she had no recollection of her father saying much, apart from an occasional suggestion to "ask your mother." The pecking order in the Chadwick home was clear.

It was Mrs. Chadwick's somewhat outdated and unfashionable view that her daughters would be just as well to find suitable husbands as go to college. She was staunchly conservative, and clung obdurately to a traditional attitude that called to a bygone era. And if a woman felt drawn so strongly to the calling of higher learning, she should at least select a college with a good medical school, where a potential husband could be sought, as a backup plan.

Helen Chadwick had bigger, or at least more independent, plans for her life. She wasn't interested in a cushy lifestyle supplied by a busy Internist with bedside manners. What she wanted was a career, something useful to do with those organizational skills that earned her the nickname "Commandant" in her senior year of high school—a title she was quietly proud of, despite the disparaging intent. So she left the family home for Toronto, and enrolled at Ryerson, in the Hospitality and Tourism Management program. She supported herself by waitressing at a busy pub near the campus.

But even the best laid plan can be derailed by a single unexpected event. Helen's goal to eventually manage a five-star hotel changed irrevocably after she served a pitcher of beer to a handsome sophomore named Mitch Doyle. Mitch was a clean-cut and charming business student whose prospects Helen found irresistible for reasons her mother would have disapproved of. They were wed a month after graduation and Helen never worked a day in her chosen field. She was her mother's daughter, after all.

Twenty-eight years and six children later, she manages the Doyle household with her favourite tool: the list. Her day cannot begin without a list. Her first list of the day is a list of all the lists she must make in order to get through the day. The grocery list will go into her purse. The drug store list will go into her husband's briefcase. He will get a small note slipped into his shirt pocket, reminding him to check the list in his briefcase. Many of the Doyle monkeys will get lists inserted into their lunch bags: things to remember to bring home from school, reminders of music or swimming lessons, general advice to the younger ones such as, "Look both ways when crossing the street."

Without her lists, Helen Doyle spirals toward insanity. As it is, the monkeys are constantly reminded that they are but one misdeed away from sending her to the Booby Hatch, a threat that none takes seriously. Lem has offered to drive her to the Booby Hatch if she feels she cannot cope; he has recently acquired a driver's license and is eager for any excuse to use it. His mother has no sense of humour.

Danny is not exempt from the barrage of daily lists. *Return video; take Peck to McVeigh's for play date after school; put dirty clothes in hamper before 8 a.m.; eat something besides fries at lunch.*

"I didn't watch the video," Danny complains. "Why should I return it?"

"You walk right by the store on your way to school."

"That's not the point."

"For Christ's sake," says Mr. Doyle. He has less tolerance than Mrs. Doyle for complaints.

"And I can't take Peck to McVeigh's. I have drama club after school."

Mrs. Doyle rummages through a stack of lists to see who else is available. She reassigns the task to Gary.

It is Peck's turn to complain. "I can go myself. I don't need someone to take me."

"You can't cross Broadview by yourself."

"Yes I can. I've done it."

"Not with my permission, you haven't. Gary will take you."

"Aw!" says Gary.

"I'm putting it on your list."

"Gary's only a year older than me. Why does he get to cross Broadview? It's not fair."

"Life isn't fair," says Mrs. Doyle. And she is right. Peck is discriminated against not because he is too young to cross a busy street alone, but because he is the youngest. In the coming years, Peck will discover that there are some benefits to being the youngest, but for now he is offended.

"Danny, you can pick up Peck from McVeigh's on your way home, then. Give me your list." She makes the adjustment to Danny's list, then scans the kitchen for Toby. "Toby, I want you to take those games back to Trevor's house. That bag has been sitting in the front hall for two weeks and I want it out of here today. Understand?"

Toby is twisting Carter's arm in an unnatural fashion. He doesn't answer, which for him is as good as affirmation.

"Don't ignore your list, Toby. And don't throw it away with the bag."

He pulls up sharply on Carter's thin arm, causing a satisfactory squawk.

"Can it, Carter," says Mr. Doyle. He doesn't care who does what to whom, or what gets broken, provided it gets done quietly. He is fighting a losing battle.

I roll over on the warm mat and look at Raymond. I need to make a list, jot down some details of my burgeoning plan. "Do you have a pen?"

"Nope."

The noise from the gymnasium dwindles. The girls' basketball team is going to the showers. The bell will ring shortly.

Raymond sits up. "I think you're taking this whole Frank thing too seriously. In three months, you'll never see him again. Don't do something you're just going to regret."

I take this opportunity to introduce an important new topic that relates to our current discussion. "Did you read the paper, this morning?"

"Yeah, right." Raymond watches cartoons during the breakfast hour, when he should be informing himself with relevant issues of the day. His parents encourage this childishness with their leniency.

"Another martyr for the Palestinian cause has blown up a bus in Hebron."

"Bunch of crazy fuckers."

"That depends on your point of view. The editorial columns are filled with heartfelt pleas for peace in the Middle East. We westerners wonder why we can't all live in peace and harmony."

"I've wondered that, myself."

"Precisely. We can't understand how an eleven-year-old boy can get a hold of a rifle in the first place, never mind find an enemy to fire it at. We shake our heads and cluck our tongues after that young boy gets cut down by return fire. We watch in wonderment as his grieving mother beats her breast and rips her hair, and then sends her nine-year-old son out into the street to pick up his brother's gun. To our sensitive eyes, the scene is anathema to our idea of childhood. And motherhood, for that matter. We can't begin to fathom the foreign mind."

"I wanted a bb-gun when I was ten, but my mother wouldn't allow it."

"Good for her." Maybe there's hope for Mrs. Dunsmore, in the end. "The point is—"

"—there's always a point, isn't there?"

"*The point is,* they have centuries of inescapable history to motivate them. No piece of land on Earth has seen more conflict than the Middle East. Everywhere they turn, they are confronted with physical and cultural reminders of endless strife. Everyone from the Romans to the Nazis have tramped across their land, taking what they want, knocking the rest down. We Canadians have no such history. We have never known foreign armies standing at our borders. Our oldest buildings are not pocked with ancient bullet strafes. We are under siege from the great American cultural juggernaut—a battle we will eventually lose, by the way—but we are not called to arms over it. We fight back by making ghastly low-budget films that win awards at

74

European film festivals. But that's nothing compared to what's gone on over there."

"The Israelites have a right to be there, too," says Raymond. He is not entirely out of the loop.

"That's for the historians to decide. What I'm trying to say is that you can't understand my need to mete out justice to Frank Dolan because you don't share my long history with him. He hasn't spent years shooting metal objects into your ears and pushing you into hedges and giving you charley horses. He hasn't spat on you and called you names and humiliated you in front of your peers. He hasn't forced you to find alternate routes to school that take you miles out of your way."

"Well," says Raymond, "I've had to do that, since I walk to school with you, most days."

"Has Frank ever laid a hand on you?"

"No."

"Has he ever said a mean thing to you?"

"He told me I was an idiot for hanging around with a loser like you."

"I think I've made my point."

"I think you've made several."

"Precisely."

The bell rings and we crawl out of our cosy crawlspace. The corridors explode with noise as two thousand students rush to fifth period. It is 12:55 and we have three minutes to get to Mrs. Stock's English class.

It seems we are going against the flow. I am jostled by shoulders, stabbed by the sharp corners of text books cradled in inconsiderate arms. I am further assaulted by a choking variety of fragrances that have been freshly applied to the girls' necks and wrists. I am marginally allergic to perfume.

As I attempt to dodge these obstacles, I am unexpectedly pressed face-first into a row of lockers, and I inhale an even more offensive odour: halitosis. One strong arm presses my head sideways into the locker door, preventing me from seeing my attacker; another strong arm has my left arm twisted most of the way up my back. I cannot move, do not dare try. I don't need to see his face to make a positive identification: Vick Peterman has just found me.

"Who the fuck are you?" he says, into the back of my neck.

Sensing that the question is rhetorical, I do not answer him.

"Who said you could touch my girlfriend?"

Another rhetorical question.

"Who said you could even *look* at my girlfriend? Answer me!"

"Who's your girlfriend?" I am stalling, hoping that a teacher might pass by and intervene.

"Every asshole with half a brain knows who my girlfriend is."

"Sorry, but I have a *whole* brain."

The upward pressure on my arm escalates. My mother is not the only one without a sense of humour.

"I'm going to crack your fucking skull open and feed your puny brain to my dog."

I try a different tack. "I think you've been misled," I say. "Whatever you've heard, it must be wrong. Look at me. Why would Marion be interested in someone like me?" As a defensive manoeuvre, self-deprecation can be useful.

"I ought to break your arm just for saying her name."

"Actually, I know more than one Marion. In fact, I have a cousin named—" My head is slammed into the locker. For a moment, I see only in black and white.

"Shut up, you little pecker. This is the only warning you're going to get. Stay away from my girlfriend."

"I thought you broke up." I should have known better. My forehead hits the locker again. Everything turns grainy.

"If I catch you even thinking about her, I'll turn you inside out and stuff you in a shoe box."

"Save it for practice," says Coach Fenchurch. I hear his sneakers retreating toward the gymnasium. In my experience, all gym teachers began life as bullies. He will be no help to me.

Vick ignores Coach Fenchurch. "If I see your ugly face again, I'm going to break your goddamned arms off and stuff them up your ass." After so many years of picking on the geeks, he has a passable repertoire of violent threats, and he can speak them with conviction.

"Okay, Vick, that sounds fair enough." I know from my own long experience as a victim that, ultimately, complete submission is the only thing that works. I don't feel ashamed for conceding. I look forward to my twenty-year reunion; we shall see who arrives in a Jaguar. I sense Vick's grip on me lessen. And then the détente falters.

"Vick, you jerk! What are you doing to him?"

That was Marion Dalton, with her impeccable timing.

"It's okay, Marion," I say, quickly. "It's nothing." My head is slammed into the locker for a third time. I'm pretty sure I see tiny yellow birds circling my head, singing *coo-tweet*.

"I warned you about saying my girlfriend's name, you little twat."

"Cut it out, Vick," shouts Marion. "You're such an asshole. No wonder I broke up with you."

"I don't accept your breakup," he shouts into my ear, meaning to direct it to Marion, I presume.

"What's that supposed to mean?" she says.

"It means that I love you, even though you're a two-timing whore and a bitch."

"You show your love with your fists, you stupid ape."

"Whatever works, darling."

I begin to feel like an intruder, but I dare not interrupt.

"Besides," says Marion, "I never cheated on you."

"What about that guy from the record shop?"

"He doesn't count. He was only a clerk."

"Jesus Christ, Marion. What does that have to do with sleeping with him?"

She huffs. "I explained it all to you before. I don't see why I have to repeat myself all the time."

"And there was that friend of your dad's. What about him?"

"I don't have to take this. We're over, Vick. You better get it through your dumb head. I'm not your girlfriend."

"We'll see about that." He presses his full weight into me. Misplaced anger.

Marion remembers that I am there. "Leave him alone. What are you going to do, Vick, beat up every boy who looks at me?"

"Come to think of it, I was just explaining that very thing to this little twerp. He was having trouble understanding, so I've promised him a couple of broken arms. I think that might help him get it. What do you think, Marion? Maybe you want to give him a good-bye kiss before I split his lip."

"I'll kiss who I like, when I like. I've got them lined up like ducks, Mister Showoff. Picking on Danny is just your way of making up for having a small dick."

I don't think that sort of comment will be helpful. I am further surprised to note that Marion remembers my name. Under better circumstances, I might be impressed. Before I can have another thought, I am shoved away, fall gracelessly to the floor. I can hardly move while I wait for the circulation to return to vital parts of my body.

"Why don't I just split *your* lip, instead?" Vick takes a step toward Marion.

"Don't, Vick!" I shout. I cannot abide men who hit women. I keep up with the news, so I know I am rare in that sentiment. A brilliantly striped Nike connects with my side.

"Listen to the mouse squeak." He laughs, and spits on me.

A moment later I see a blur in my peripheral vision, and there is a loud crash, as Vick is pushed headlong into the lockers. Where my head had struck the locker door in the center, a relative soft spot, Vick's forehead went straight for the joist. It was a solid connection that could be heard even above the rattling combination locks and Marion's shriek.

Raymond has come to my rescue, blindsiding Vick and bravely putting himself in harm's way. I am proud of him. I was beginning to wonder what became of him. Perhaps I have miscalculated his athletic prowess, after all.

Bedlam ensues as the noise finally attracts the faculty. They do not come out of their holes unless they think school property is being destroyed. The configuration is now reversed: I am standing while Vick lies on the ground, gripping his head. Raymond stands beside me, panting, and Marion is backing away. All the witnesses are fleeing the scene, and Raymond has the same idea. "C'mon, let's go, man." He grabs me by the shirt, but I resist. A handful of teachers arrives, can't get a handle on the situation. They hover over Vick Peterman and wonder who or what could have done this to him. They would never believe the truth.

I permit Raymond to take me away.

"Don't look back," he says, pulling me along. The late bell has just rung.

"Thanks, Ray." For the moment, I need not say more to my best friend.

"Don't call me Ray."

We duck into Mrs. Stock's English class, the last to arrive.

Chapter 8

I came to understand at an early age that I was special.

My Aunt Joy, the plump and timid youngest of my mother's family, was the first to openly acknowledge this. She called me "precocious," and once she defined the word for me, I had to agree.

"You're a smart little boy," she said.

I objected only to being called "little."

My parents have an established pattern of sending members of their brood away for as much of the summer vacation as they can legally get away with. If they can't find suitable camps to incarcerate us in, they turn to far-flung relatives to take up the slack. Aunt Joy took me for an interminable six-week stretch when I was ten. By then, I was reading Kurt Vonnegut. No wonder she was impressed.

Aunt Joy lives alone in the old Victorian house she and my mother grew up in. She has never lived outside Fenlon Falls, indeed has never lived in any other house, and even back then, when she took me for that long summer, she was well on her way to spinsterhood. She will never marry because she has no self-esteem—a shortcoming that makes her very agreeable company.

"I hope you're not too bored, way out here in the middle of nowhere, with an old lady like me," she said to me on my first day there.

I have just calculated that she would have been in her late twenties; hardly Noachian. Of course, now, seven years later, she is of an age beyond redemption. She made her apology because I was originally slated to arrive with along with one of the monkeys. At the last moment my aunt realized that she might not be able to "handle" two rambunctious boys, so the monkey was redirected to Cadets. Poor bastard.

"You can swim at the public beach, and there are plenty of other places you can walk to. Nothing is very far." Aunt Joy does not drive. "And there are lots of other children in town. Don't be shy about making friends, Danny. You'll be here all summer. It will be nice if you made a friend or two. Just don't play near the locks. We lost a boy there, last summer. A terrible tragedy." The citizens of Fenlon Falls will never let you forget their importance in the Trent Severn Waterway system—a vital thoroughfare and, apparently, a killer of unwary boys.

Thus warned, I spent long hours at the locks, tossing pebbles into the cockpits of the descending boats. And I live to tell the story. I avoided the public beach; it was full of obnoxious tourists and their squealing offspring. I easily adopted the prevailing local attitude toward the summer cottagers and tourists, which was that they were uncivilized interlopers, ignorant of all things "north," and were therefore to be viewed with a form of mild scorn mixed with a dose of pity. Technically I was a resident, so was qualified to shake my head and cluck my tongue at these garish city-slickers.

There were only two traffic lights in Fenlon Falls, and they were sufficiently ill-timed as to make the town seem a thriving bucolic landmark, where in fact all that traffic was merely an endless snake of frustrated and over-heated travellers, cursing the town planners and plotting an alternate route for the journey home. There was little in Fenlon Falls to interest a boy of ten. Most of the shops on Main Street were designed to bilk the tourists.

The town had a cinema that ran the latest blockbusters, three months late. I loitered under the marquee, admiring the action-packed posters and scrutinizing the exiting crowds for signs of disappointment. Lack of funds prevented me from attending a single movie. My mother sent me north with the meager contents of my piggy-bank—another intended lesson for yours truly. Apart from a pocket full of jangling coins, I had no money of my own. So each morning Aunt Joy gave me a five dollar bill to get me through the day. "Coke money," she called it. "A boy shouldn't wander the streets penniless." I was grateful for the gift, but five dollars wasn't enough money to get me into a show, and I couldn't bring myself to ask for more. She was already so nervous about her responsibility for me that I couldn't add a financial burden on top of it.

When I wasn't wasting the day at the locks, I spent long hours in

Aunt Joy's expansive back yard. Hers was one of the few original properties that hadn't been severed. In back stood ancient oak and maple trees, enticing in their size and shape for boys who are inclined to climb. If I wasn't attempting to conquer a sixty-foot maple, I was swinging on the old whitewall that hung from its thickest limb. A broad spectrum of local wildlife was represented in that yard. Woodpeckers and blue jays and finches flitted through the green canopy overhead. A family of plump raccoons sat quietly in a row on one of the taller branches, watching my tentative ascension. When I got too close, the mother screeched at me, and the family scuttled further upward, out of reach. Crows scrawed and cicadas whined, but it was the multitude of chipmunks that intrigued me most.

"My neighbour feeds them," said Aunt Joy. There was disapproval in her tone. "Ever since his old dog died, he's been putting nuts out for them. I can't even begin to count them this year."

I tried counting them, myself. I stopped at twenty. I couldn't be sure I wasn't counting the same ones twice.

It was clear the subject was a sore one for Aunt Joy, and she was too polite to confront her lonely neighbour over the issue. "Sometimes I wish he'd just get himself another dog, but, frankly, I wasn't overwrought after Samson passed on. You can appreciate the peaceful nights we have around here, now that we don't have that old thing barking at the moon."

I could not entice the chipmunks to take a peanut from my palm, no matter how desperate they were to have it. They were seized by spasms of flight, mixed with brief moments of terrified stupor. Their skittishness entranced me. I made a game of seeing how close I could get to one before it fled in a fit of panic. After a while, the futility of my efforts motivated me to improve my reach by brandishing a stick. I approached my target with great stealth, barely daring to breathe. The chipmunk was not fooled. It knew that danger was near. Its small black eyes nearly popped out of its head as it weighed the situation. It was clinging to the base of the maple tree.

A blink later the chipmunk was on the ground, motionless. My stick had come down with greater swiftness than I expected. I made a direct hit. I looked down on the rodent, unsure if it was dead or just stunned. I was afraid it might leap up and bite my neck—an irrational fear, I knew. I was even more afraid that I had killed it. I am cursed with a deep and vigorous conscience.

I poked the animal with the stick, and when it failed to respond I threw the stick away and ran back to the locks, where I spent the remainder of the morning crying, and throwing larger-than-usual pebbles with more-than-usual force at the boats. Finally, the lockmaster shooed me away with a string of unprofessional oaths.

I confessed to the crime. Aunt Joy was typically understanding, although I could see, beneath the compassionate veneer, that she was troubled by the apparent violence of the deed. Having known only sisters, she did not understand what my mother refers to as "boy energy," a clever and useful euphemism for the male capacity for thoughtless brutality.

"You probably did me a favour, Danny, but I can't recommend your methods."

I took her out back to show her the corpse, but it was gone.

"Maybe some other animal ate it," I said. Boys, I find, have a tendency to fancy the morbid thoughts first.

"You probably just knocked it silly. It came round after you left. It's probably up in my attic right now, eating my insulation," she said, wryly.

I nodded. I liked her explanation better than mine.

During the quiet evenings after dinner we played Scrabble. I never lost a game. I was only ten, so I could easily suspect my aunt of throwing her game, but I believe I held my own.

"You have an impressive vocabulary," she said.

I had just laid down *expiate* for a triple-word score.

Danny Doyle made only one friend that summer in Fenlon Falls: a boy named Scout, two years his senior. In later years Joy would reflect that it was a stroke of misfortune that Danny had to befriend the wickedest boy in town, an assessment that was perhaps exaggerated, but not completely without warrant. Scout Findlay was bursting with "boy energy."

The two boys met at Arcadia, a dark cavern stuffed with an antiquated collection of arcade games, a virtual museum that included Pac-Man and Galaga. At the rear of the long, narrow space stood a pool table, rarely used by the young boys who congregated at Arcadia because it didn't plug into a wall socket and couldn't be played with a joystick.

"What are you doing here?" Scout asked, leaning against the

unused pool table, watching the ten-year-old newcomer as he made his way to the back.

"Playing," said Danny. Which was not exactly true. He had not yet given up any of his precious coins to these old games.

"Everything here is shit. Let's go to my house."

How easily childhood friendships are made; so often the only requirement is *availability*.

"I haven't seen you around."

"I live in Toronto. I'm just here for the summer, with my aunt."

"Tough break."

"Yeah."

"There's nothing to do in this dump."

He needed to impress the older boy. "I killed a chipmunk, yesterday."

Scout's interest piqued. "How'd you do it?"

"With a stick."

"There's better ways than that," said Scout.

The Findlays lived on the perimeter of town. Theirs was the last residence on the road leading north to Haliburton. The house itself looked unfinished, a ramshackle bungalow with tarpaper stapled to the north side, forlornly awaiting final dressing. At the end of the driveway sat a '67 Firebird, faded orange with a hem of rust and a hand-painted For Sale sign angled over the windshield. Danny had already noted that "up north," everything was for sale. In back, there were a half-dozen more vehicles in various stages of decomposition. Also in the rear was a cinderblock structure that was not quite a garage and not quite a barn. It had a large roll-up door, plus a regular door, two small windows and a flat roof. Flashes of light flared through the windows.

"My dad's a welder," said Scout.

They peered through the window so Danny could be impressed. It was a monstrous and powerful image to him: the black-clad man in the mask, shooting brilliant bolts of lightning at all that steel. It was a profound picture for the youngster whose own father's ill-equipped toolbox languished in the basement with the price tags still intact.

"Don't look at the light or you'll go blind," said Scout.

Danny blinked, rubbed his eyes. The advice had come a bit late.

After a suitable length of time they left Scout's father to his work and entered the house. The back door led to a kitchen that redefined disorder for Danny. He was fairly certain a germ couldn't have survived in that environment. He breathed through his mouth and tried not to look directly at any of the surfaces. Scout led him down a dim corridor, to a small room, where the disarray took on a whole new dimension. The room seemed to serve multi-purposes, as a warehouse, a workshop, a playground, a greenhouse, a garage. Somewhere in there was a bed, the ostensible function of the room. The room smelled of gasoline and damp grass.

Danny Doyle had seen what six bored boys could do to a room on a rainy Saturday afternoon, but he had seen nothing like this before. "You sleep in here?" His tone was mildly disparaging.

Scout shrugged and stepped over a half-built go-kart in order to reach the closet.

Danny's bedroom, back in Toronto, was a model of tidiness. He needed no prompting from his mother to clean his room; he cannot exist in chaos. Dado needs things to be in their proper place.

Rummaging in the closet, Scout toppled boxes and sporting equipment and sundry miscellany. At last, he found what he was looking for.

"This is better than a fucking stick," he said. He levelled a small rifle at Danny.

"Cool," said Danny. He had never seen a real gun.

"My dad calls it the rat catcher. It shoots pellets, but it can take out a squirrel, no problem. Or a chipmunk."

"Cool."

"You can kill a cat with it, but you have to shoot it a bunch of times."

"Right."

"Want to try it?"

"Maybe we could shoot some tin cans, or something."

Scout laughed. "Yeah, right."

Guns have never been permitted in my house. I don't think my mother took a moral stand against firearms, so much as she understood that with six boys running loose, the presence of such a weapon could only increase the likelihood of an accident, thus upsetting the precarious balance of her daily schedule. She can deal with the cuts and bruises as they come, but she does not relish wasting a valuable afternoon rushing one of her little ones to the emergency ward with a hole in his eye. As it is, she is kept busy by Carter, who is prone to injuries, often due to his proximity to Toby. Carter has broken both legs and two fingers, suffered a small fracture in his skull, dislocated his left shoulder (thank Toby again) and carries a metal pin in one of his elbows. One recent incident involved the unexplained adhesion, by super-glue, of a Star Wars action figure to the center of his forehead. We all suspect Toby.

Standing in Scout's bedroom, cradling the pellet rifle in my arms, I felt a dangerous thrill and an ominous sense of foreboding. I was a sensible kid who knew right from wrong better than most ten-year-olds, yet I was drawn to the powerful potential of this simple piece of hardware. In my hands I held *death*.

"Let's go," said Scout.

Across a field we trudged, headed for a copse that bordered a field of budding corn. The midday sun caused me to squint. I was permitted to carry the rifle for the cross-field journey, but once we reached the trees, Scout reclaimed it. He would have the first shot—a proprietary perk.

"See anything?" he asked, peering into the branches overhead.

"No."

We stood still. The wind blew our hair. We were a quarter mile south of Scout's house. We could see the highway to the east. There was open field to the north, and the verge of a dense pine forest to the west, from which the copse protruded like a finger. We were alone.

Scout raised the rifle, taking aim. "Here we go."

I couldn't see what he was aiming at. I tried to follow the trajectory, but saw nothing except trees. When he pulled the trigger, the report was small, not what I expected; more of a *clack* than a *bang*. I remembered it was only a pellet gun. I saw something move quickly around the tree trunk: a black squirrel.

"Missed the fucker," Scout said.

"My turn," I said. But I was not familiar with the rules of fair gunplay.

"Wait. I didn't get him, yet." He firmed his stance, kept his aim.

This time I could see the squirrel, watched its nervous movements. It raised its nose in the air, sniffing. It knew that danger lurked. For a squirrel, danger is everywhere. Danger waited patiently for a clear shot. Two quick steps up the trunk and the rodent was within range. It sniffed constantly, putting its nose forward to taste the air. Every move the squirrel made was one of nervous terror. In a blur, it moved several feet back down the tree and stopped, this time facing us directly, completely exposed.

The rifle *clacked!* I flinched. At first it seemed as if the critter had dodged another bullet. With tremendous speed, it moved downward. I could hear the click of its claws as they grappled for a hold on the bark, but its movements were faltering. It froze for a moment, and then dropped to the ground.

"Got him!" shouted Scout.

We rushed to the tree to inspect our quarry. The squirrel was still alive, but could not run away. It wriggled in the long grass as if jolted by unseen bolts of electricity, as if it were being *welded*. It screamed, called for help, perhaps was warning others away.

"What do we do now?" I asked. It was a life-and-death question.

"Watch."

I watched. "Do you think it's in pain?"

"Sure. Animals feel things just the same as us."

I didn't like his answer. I remembered how badly I felt after I thought I'd killed the chipmunk in Aunt Joy's backyard. I didn't enjoy watching this one suffer. "How long is this going to take?"

"You got something else to do?"

"No. I was just wondering."

"You'll get your turn. Don't worry."

I was no longer keen to wield the power of life and death. I wanted to go home. I wanted to play cards with my aunt or read a book. I would rather lean on the railing at the locks and watch the boats go up and down. But I was here. I was committed.

Dado missed the shot.

It may have been the wind, buffeting through the copse. It may have been the sun in his eyes. It may also have been a conscience asserting itself. In any case, the pellets chipped away at the bark and did no worse damage than that.

Several weeks of reckless pre-pubescent competition ensued, much involving motorcycles or power tools or the scaling of sheer and crumbling rock faces at the base of the locks; after which Danny Doyle ditched the delinquent Scout, avoided the influence of an older boy who should have known better, and somehow survived his time with Aunt Joy.

When I think back to that summer, I sense that other forces were at work around me. Within me. The incident in Aunt Joy's backyard, stalking the chipmunk with a stick, is a vivid memory for me, except for the moment when I actually struck the unlucky animal. Those few seconds are blank. I remember seeing the chipmunk lying on the grass, seemingly dead. At the time, my brain must have filled in those missing seconds, but now, as I think back with a clearer head, I begin to suspect that Dog has been meddling again. Sometimes his voice sounds remarkably like mine.

I cannot always trust my inner voice.

Chapter 9

Peck is following in my footsteps. He is only in grade three, and already he has been targeted by a schoolyard bully: a fourth-grader named Neville.

One night recently, we are in our respective beds, lights out, moonlit shadows waving across the ceiling. He should have been asleep hours ago, but he is troubled. "He took my lunch away and stepped on it," says Peck.

"Why?"

"I don't know."

"Did you look at him?"

"No."

"That's a problem. Bullies don't like to be ignored. You have to at least make eye contact."

"He punched Steve for looking at him the other day."

"Well, there's an art to making eye contact with bullies without actually looking at them. You have to practice it."

"I don't know."

"It works to fend off the lunatics, too."

"They don't bother me."

"Anyway, ignoring bullies is always a bad idea. They take it as an insult. Neville probably just wants attention, and doesn't know how to get it in a positive way. I imagine he's sensitive about his name."

"Some of the grade-sixers call him *Navel*."

"Naturally."

For years I shared my room with Lem. After pubescence took hold of him, his masturbatory fervour wore me down until I traded him in for a younger model. By the time Peck discovers the wide usage of his left hand (he is the only southpaw in the house), I will be long gone. The downside to my young roomie is his disinclination to clean up after himself. Since, by eleven-thirty, when I retire to bed, our room is dark, I am forever stepping on small, sharp toys that have been abandoned in the middle of the floor. Peck is good-natured and shows promise intellectually, but he lacks discipline.

"For Christ's sake," I shout, hopping around in the dark, clutching my sore foot. "Put this shit away!"

He feigns sleep, deaf to my rebuke. This is my mother's fault. By the time Peck came along, she lost interest in instilling her children with good habits and solid values. After squeezing out six boys, she can do no more than feed them and keep them out of traffic. The only exception to this condensed philosophy relates to the potty training the youngest four monkeys underwent. To this day, they do not know that other boys pee standing up. Since my mother bears full responsibility for cleaning the bathroom, she can be forgiven this license. Seven culprits with bad aim are more than she can take.

Once I've perfected the invisibility thing, I'll pass the technique on to Peck. In the meantime, I'll do what I can to help him with his bully problem.

"First of all," I tell him, "if you want Neville to ignore you, you have to stop dawdling."

"I don't dawdle," says Peck.

"Yes, you do."

"No, I don't. What's dawdle mean?"

"For Christ's sake."

"Language."

"Do you want my help or not?"

I hear a soft asthmatic sound from across the room. Peck is sucking the corner of his pillow slip. His oral fixation is relentless.

"You have to stop picking up every pebble on the sidewalk."

"I don't."

"You do. You put them in your mouth. It's a filthy habit. It's a wonder you're not sick more often, considering the things you put in your mouth."

"Sometimes I just put them in my pocket."

"If Neville slugs you when you've got a pebble in your mouth, you're liable to choke to death."

I already know that the threat of death means nothing to Peck. When our cat Zippo keeled over dead, last year (prematurely, in my estimation—I suspect a suicide), Peck spent months writing letters to the dead cat, dropping them into the post box and assuming they would be delivered in a timely manner. Naturally, he complained that Zippo failed to write back; and even after I explained, again, all the various symptoms and consequences of death to Peck—not to mention the fact that, as a cat, Zippo's writing skills would be rudimentary, at best—he responded to Zippo's rudeness: "That's no excuse for not writing." I fear my little brother hasn't yet figured out death, so the threat of it will have no impact on him.

"I don't put them all in my mouth."

"You're missing the point, Peck. It's the dawdling that's going to get you hit."

"What's dawdling, again?"

I sigh. "Dawdling is when you shuffle along slowly, stopping all the time to pick things up—"

"—like pebbles?"

"Yes, like pebbles. When you walk, you need to go at a crisp and steady pace, as if you're nearly late for something, but not rushing."

"What?"

"Walk fast. Pretend you're late."

"I usually am late."

"That's because you dawdle."

"I don't pick up all the pebbles."

"Forget the bottle caps, too." Peck has had two tetanus shots, thanks to a dirty and pointless collection of rusty bottle caps he keeps under his bed.

"I collect them."

"I know you do. What do you do with them, once you've collected them?"

"I don't know. Look at them, I guess."

"You leave them spilled on the floor, and then you step on them with your bare feet and cut yourself. Remember the needles you had to get?"

"Yes," he says, quietly. They were painful needles.

"They're dirty, and they smell like stale root beer."

"They don't smell."

"Anyway, why don't you collect baseball cards, like all the other kids your age?"

"Baseball's boring."

"Unlike a box full of dirty, smelly bottle caps that have provided you with absolutely no fun, whatsoever, and have actually caused you a great deal of pain? You need to get your priorities in order, little man."

"What's priorities?"

"Right. So walk fast, and look at Neville without looking at him. That's the trick."

"How do I look at him without looking at him?"

"Well, you pass your eyes across his, but you focus on something behind him."

"Like what?"

"I don't know. Anything. The wall. A tree. Whatever's back there."

"You don't have to get mad."

"I'm not mad."

"You're huffy."

"I'm not huffy. I'm trying to help you, but you're not making it easy."

"I can cross Broadview by myself," he says. Like Raymond, when he feels he is getting nowhere he changes the subject.

"I know."

"Mom treats me like a little kid."

"You are a little kid. Mom worries about you because you dawdle."

"I don't dawdle." He has heard nothing I've said.

"She's afraid you're going to stop in the middle of Broadview to pick up a pebble and get hit by a bus."

"It hasn't happened, yet."

"Precisely." The room falls silent. I shut my eyes and the darkness hardly changes. I know that Peck is not asleep because he snores. "Why do you do it?" I ask.

"What?"

"Why do you put pebbles in your mouth?"

"Mom won't give me money for candy."

"Don't they taste awful?"

"What do you mean?"

"What do you mean 'What do you mean?' I mean, don't the pebbles taste like dirt?"

"I don't know what dirt tastes like."

"What do the pebbles taste like?"

"Nothing, really."

"Nothing? They must taste like something."

"Like everything else. But harder."

I begin to suspect something. "Doesn't a peppermint candy taste better than a pebble?"

"I don't know."

"What about chocolate?"

"It's softer. Pebbles last longer."

I am beginning to understand. "Tell me something. Remember when Toby sat on your head and farted?"

"Which time?"

"I don't know. Any time."

"Yeah."

"What was it like?"

"Not very nice. It hurt when he sat on my head."

"He farted right in your face."

"That wasn't very nice, either."

"Did it smell?"

"I don't know."

I have learned something new about my brother that answers a number of questions. Another long silence passes between us.

"Danny?"

"Yes?"

"I have to go pee."

"Go ahead. But remember what I told you about standing up."

I hear his small feet land on the carpet, move toward the door. "Mom said I'm not supposed to listen to you. She says you're joking."

I am resigned.

Chapter 10

The atmosphere in Mrs. Stock's English class is muted, like a narrow residential street after a thick snowfall. As always, Raymond and I sit at the back of the classroom. My breathing is heavy, my system shot with adrenaline after my altercation with Vick Peterman.

"Thanks, Ray." He has proved a loyal friend. One day I will return the favour.

My friend is likewise flushed and breathless. Otherwise he would surely admonish me for calling him Ray. "No problem."

"Ever since Marion dumped him, he's been a loose cannon." The geeks have had it pretty rough for the past month. "It's bad enough that I have Frank lurking over my shoulder. Now I have to watch out for the goddamned jocks, too." I wonder if I should put my plans for Frank on hold until after the Vick situation cools down. But I have made the oath. I have made the plan. And somewhere below the surface I know that if I wait, I will change my mind. Even if Dog is manipulating me, as he is wont to do, I will use it to my advantage, use Dog's strength to make me stronger.

I am resigned.

I engage in Mrs. Stock's lesson, grateful for the distraction.

"I trust you've all finished reading *The Cider House Rules* by now," she says, leaning on the front edge of her desk. There is nothing indeterminate about her age, or her attractiveness. Mrs. Stock is on the far side of middle age, matronly, soft-spoken. She displays Herculean patience for the illiterate boobs who populate her classroom, a group for which I have nothing but scorn. She gives passing grades to those students who are willing to put in the effort, even if they continue to split infinitives and misplace intransitive verbs.

Several desks creak. Those students who have not read the book shift uncomfortably.

"How many of you," she continues, aware of the nervous shifts, "rented the movie rather than read the book?" She gives them a fair chance to come clean before she takes them to task.

Four honest hands go up. I sense that there were a further ten elbows that jerked, but did not rise.

Mrs. Stock holds up her copy of the thick novel. "Five hundred and ninety-eight single-spaced pages of small type," she says. "The film script was probably something like two-hundred-and-forty pages, double-spaced, typed in a courier font that requires fifteen-percent more room than Times Roman."

She pauses in order to let those statistics sink in.

"How many of you have actually read the entire novel?"

Six hands go up, including mine. Out of the corner of my eye I see Raymond's arm twitch, but his hands rest flaccidly on his desk, like two dead fish. I give him the *eye,* and he shrugs.

Mrs. Stock does not seem surprised by these results. She has been around nearly as long as Mr. Bukowski and Mr. Seale. "Have any of you seen the movie *and* read the entire book?"

Mine is the only hand remaining raised. I finished the book before I rented the movie, so, naturally, I was disappointed by the screen adaptation.

Mrs. Stock acknowledges my thoroughness. "Do you have an opinion of the movie, Danny?" My English teacher is well aware that I have an opinion about everything.

"Typical sub-standard fare from Hollywood," I say.

"Can you elaborate, please?"

"There were some good casting choices, and the cinematography was splendid, but apart from that, the film falls considerably short of the book. When one is condensing a novel for the screen, especially a long novel like this one, it's widely accepted that cuts must be made. Secondary characters and minor sub-plots are eliminated. It's an unfortunate truth that the movie studios resist a film longer than two hours, so these manipulations of the story are the rule more than the exception. But this movie's greatest crime against the book is the development of the relationship between Homer Wells and Candy Kendall. In the book, the romance transpires after Candy's fiancé,

94

Wally, is shot down over Burma and declared missing in action. They all believe he is dead. So when Wally unexpectedly turns up very much alive, an uncomfortable situation arises. But it's an *honest* situation. In the movie, Candy Kendall's motivation for having an affair with Homer is, at best, flimsy. She comes across as immature and selfish. Instead of being portrayed as a grieving widow, she is reduced to a faithless trollop, unworthy of either man. They try to gloss over it with a sweeping musical score and some soft lighting, but she is still just a two-timing hussy. Instead of feeling Homer's angst at leaving her behind with a cuckolded paraplegic, I was relieved that he got away from her onerous clutches." My father hated the movie because there was too much kissing in it.

Mrs. Stock scans the room. Most of my classmates avoid eye contact. "Who can sum up the meaning of the book in one sentence?"

A thick silence descends on the room.

"War is bad?" offers Mindy Petrich, tentatively. She is not an A student.

"Anyone else?" From Mrs. Stock, two simple words can cut deeper than a tirade about the prevalent stupidity of today's youth.

"Abortion is bad?" says Helen Fawcett. I doubt she read past the first chapter. She is a reborn Christian.

Mrs. Stock passes a pleading glance in my direction. Once again I must save the moment, spare my peers further humiliation. "We cannot ignore our chosen destiny," I say.

"Okay. Now we're getting somewhere. Can anyone expand on that?"

I lean over to Raymond to have a private conversation. "You've had a month to read that book," I whisper.

"I was going for a high score in Wave Race."

"Jesus, Ray. You need to get rid of the Nintendo before it's too late."

"It's good for the hand-eye coordination."

"You won't have any use for your hands or your eyes, once your brain melts."

He rolls his eyes. "Thanks, Mom."

"Don't compare me to her. I'm trying to *help* you."

"I shouldn't be taking advice from someone who's trying to get a gun so he can kill someone."

I *shush* him, look around to see if anyone overheard. "Keep your voice down, you idiot. Are you trying to get me arrested?"

His ears burn red.

"Anyway, we're talking about your lack of scholastic responsibility."

"I'd rather not."

"No doubt. But just look at your handwriting. It's gotten noticeably worse, lately. You're probably getting carpal tunnel syndrome."

"I got the high score, though. It was worth it."

"There's no practical value to those games, Ray. Hand-eye coordination will not help you as an insurance salesman for State Farm."

"Very funny." Raymond cannot see his own destiny. "I saved you from Vick. Remember? I think you should stop nagging me for the rest of the day. You're in some kind of mood."

"My work is never done."

"Is there something you wish to add to the conversation, Danny?" Mrs. Stock is a vigilant teacher.

"No, ma'am. I've made my point."

"Perhaps you care to listen to someone else's point of view, then."

"Yes, ma'am."

Some days I feel unappreciated.

Dado opens his notebook. Now is the time to make his list. He poises the pencil over the blank page, then reconsiders. Should he leave evidence of his plan? Is he wise to rely on the Young Offender's Act to protect him from a life sentence? A new plan, one that doesn't involve a gun, might enable him to achieve the desired result without facing a murder rap. If Frank's death looks like an accident, Danny's involvement might not even be suspected. Raymond's idea to scare Frank into submission is admittedly a good one. At times, his friend shows a glimmer of intelligence, thinks Danny. If only he would apply himself. But perhaps Dado has made a calculated error by discussing his plan with Raymond. Can he be trusted to keep his mouth shut? Perhaps Raymond should be more deeply involved; that will encourage his silence. Make him an accomplice. Or make him a victim—

Shut up, Dog! I know it's you, putting these bad thoughts in my head.

I know that Dog is real because I am not crazy. I have checked and double-checked; I have done the research and concluded that I am more sane than most people. If Dog were a delusion, a diabolical fragment of a damaged mind, there would be other symptoms, and there are none. I have no pathological tendencies. I am not paranoid. I know that the people who are out to get me are real. Raymond is my witness.

The plan will go forward, unwritten. Ray will help me because that's what best friends do for each other. The deed will bond us forever. And Frank Dolan will soon discover that in hell, everyone is prey.

I must use the remainder of the class to concentrate on something else, keep Dog from intruding on my thoughts. I open a small book: Romeo and Juliet. I will be Romeo in this spring's school production. We are still doing table sessions for the play, reading the scenes in character, working the text until the meaning is clear. Most of the cast are hopeless, do not understand what they are saying, will never get the hang of iambic pentameter. In the end, it will not matter. The two leads will carry the show. Heidi Borland will be my Juliet. Destiny. Full rehearsals do not begin for two more weeks and I am nearly off-book. I have a superior memory, which allows me to concentrate on my acting rather than my lines. I know everyone else's lines, too, so I am a great help to the company, although their appreciation is sometimes under-whelming.

"*You are a lover, borrow Cupid's wings—*" says Leonard Mapother, who is playing Mercutio, my (Romeo's) best friend. The only thing Leonard has going for him in this production is that he dies painfully before intermission. He cannot remember his lines.

"—*And soar with them above a common bound,*" I prompt.

"I know the line, Doyle, if you'd give me a bloody chance."

"You won't get a second chance once you're up there onstage, Leo."

"Mrs. Banks, tell Danny to stop doing that."

"You make us all look bad when you fail to do the work," I say.

"Okay, Danny," interjects Mrs. Banks.

Leonard will never be an actor unless he learns how to take notes with grace.

"I knew the next line," he lies. "It was just a dramatic pause."

"It's always dramatic for us," I say, "as we grind our teeth and wonder which line you'll forget next."

"Mrs. Banks!"

"Okay, Danny. That's enough." Mrs. Banks knows that I am right, but she must coddle Leonard as if he were a troublesome and sensitive toddler. The director's job is akin to child psychologist. "Leonard, let's try it again, this time without the dramatic pause."

Heidi Borland sits across the table from me with love in her eyes. She is in character. She is the real thing: an actor. Together, we could take the world by storm. Like Burton and Taylor. Newman and Woodward. It is a perfectly natural thing for romantic leads to come away from an intense production with genuine feelings for each other. As actors, we must draw from emotional truth if we are to give truth to our characters. I am counting on the truth of Romeo and Juliet's love to carry Heidi and me beyond the length of the run. I do not need to *act* my love for her. Our scenes are electric.

"*Let me stand here till thou remember it.*"

"*I shall forget, to have thee still stand there, remembering how I love thy company.*"

"*And I'll still stay, to have thee still forget, forgetting any other home but this.*"

Her words wash over me like a warm rain. Her eyes lock onto mine as we dance a beautiful dance of words, evoking awe from the cast and tears from Mrs. Banks. We are connected by gossamer threads that unite us as one meaningful love that cannot be broken. We shall be together like this forever.

Danny Doyle projects himself into the future. A milestone reunion is at hand. Twenty years have passed since he left his mark etched into the desktops of Laidlaw High School. Now he is returning, a glittering icon of success, an acknowledged and celebrated genius of the stage. *The New Olivier,* they call him. He will not arrive at the reunion in a Jaguar, as the geeks will; he will arrive in a limousine, piloted by a burly Italian named Salvatori. A squad of security men will cut a path through the throng of hysterical fans that pursue him, day and night, dreaming of copping a feel or snatching a valuable autograph. In an effort to stave off a riot, he permits a few of each. On his arm will be Heidi Borland, stunning in sequins and glittering with jewels. She will be Heidi Doyle now, having shucked her personal aspirations for the stage in order to support her husband. As they move toward the entrance, the crowd will part like the Red Sea, giving safe passage to the one man who can deliver to his people the promised land called Escape.

Danny Doyle, Lord of the Stage, makes the Hollywood gods seem provincial, pagan. He has set the new benchmark in popularity. He has single-handedly initiated a resurgence in theatre attendance. While the space-age multiplex cinemas languish like barren ghost towns, rush seating has become the last hope for countless fans of the great Dado who did not have the foresight to reserve tickets two years in advance.

"You look magnificent, darling," I whisper, as we glide into the gymnasium.

Hundreds of surrounding eyes will concur. "Who's the dish on Doyle's arm?" they will ask each other. "Heidi who?" They will not remember her from their Laidlaw days because she did not leave her mark on anything but my heart. In spite of her relative anonymity, she will be happy with her circumstances. We have more money and more happiness than two people deserve.

"Should I call the babysitter?" she asks, as we sit down to dinner at the head table, in the place of honour.

"Don't worry, darling," I say. "Danny Jr. is in good hands with Matilda. I'm sure everything is fine."

"I wish I could have your confidence, sweetheart."

We will kiss, a merger that will be witnessed by everyone in the gymnasium. They will applaud, envy, love, and hate us for that kiss. So be it.

After dinner, Mrs. Banks, now ancient and cracked, will stand at the microphone and give a moving tribute to me, in which she will take all the credit for my success. I will permit her this small joy. It's the least I can do in return for her having cast Heidi and me together in that fateful play, setting in motion a twenty-year love story. Mrs. Stock will also venture out of the retirement home to make a rare public appearance for my benefit. I will embrace both ladies and permit photographs to be snapped of us together. It will be a moving moment for them, the highlight of their long, dull lives.

Naturally, Marion Dalton will be there with her third husband, Paco—a jewellery store franchisee with a deep tan and a porcelain smile. Marion will be plump but stylish. Her blonde hair will be mostly artificial, as will be her smile. She will have four ungrateful children and a long history with men that puts our little hallway tryst into perspective. She will approach my table with wine-induced bravery, hug me awkwardly and brush my cheek with an airy kiss that stinks of Chanel. She will make polite small-talk as if we were the oldest of friends. She will tell me about her children, and Heidi will retaliate by telling her about our beloved son, Daniel Jr., the luckiest child yet born. But Marion's eyes will tell the sad story of an empty life, will plead with me to throw her a bone, give her a reason to live for another day.

"We had such a time, back then, didn't we, Danny?"

"By the way, Marion, you haven't changed a bit. I'd have recognized you anywhere."

She takes the bone and flees back to her table across the room, recounts to anyone drunk enough to listen how she and I were once "involved." I will take no legal action against her for this license. Over the years I have been slandered by bigger fish than her.

Throughout the evening a steady stream of geeks will approach me with: "Hey, Danny, remember me?" I will not, but I will play along. I will shake hands with their beautiful wives and nod appreciatively at their good fortunes.

"A *silver* Porsche, you say? So, you drive *yourself* around, then? How quaint."

Vick Peterman will arrive amid a few half-hearted cheers from his old crones. His hair will be salt-and-pepper, prematurely grey due to his having gone into politics. He will be a controversial city counsellor. He will lead the way in reopening the nude beach on the west shore of Toronto Island. He will be instrumental in securing prime waterfront real estate for his friends in the development sector, for which he will receive many under-the-table gifts, including a brand new car. He will not be supported by the police association because he is a Liberal. He will never rise above the municipal playing field. He will, by his own account, be a nice guy.

"Say, Danny Boy," he will croon, hand outstretched, political smile set. "Nice to see you. How long's it been?"

"Twenty years," I'll say. "At least, that's what it said on the invitation."

Vic laughs heartily. "Good one, Danny. Still have that sense of

100

humour, eh?"

"That makes one of us." Another one shot over his head.

Vic looks off into the distance. "Those were the days. You know, sometimes I wish I could go back, stay a teenager forever." He snaps out of his reverie. "Anyway, it's great to see the old gang."

"One or two notable absences," I say. I am ready for this conversation to end.

Vic's eyebrows contort. "Did you hear about Severin? Tragic. A real tragedy."

"Who is Severin?" I will ask. One man's tragedy is another man's justice.

Vick will have had twenty years to alter his memories to better suit a kind and respectable adult. He will have forgotten about his insane jealousy of Marion Dalton, which led to his assault of me. He wants to be my friend, but that is not in the cards for us. He will quickly run out of things to say to me, and then he will wander away, wondering why I am no longer his best friend.

My old best friend Raymond will, naturally, arrive late. His suit will be wrinkled and he will be buttoning his shirt collar when he shuffles through the doors. He will spot me right away in the throng because everyone does. He will wait patiently in the shadows as a clutch of geeks pays me homage.

"Hey, Danny."

I will turn to my old friend and give him the first sincere smile of the evening. "Hello, Raymond. Good to see you."

"Ray. Call me Ray."

We will laugh. Shake hands. Hug.

"Hello, Heidi." He is the only one who remembers her. "Been a long time."

"I'm going to give Matilda a quick call," Heidi will say, permitting Raymond and me a private moment to reunite.

"How was London?"

"Fine, fine," I say. "Well, dismal if you are referring to the weather, but otherwise fine. *Peer Gynt* was a smash hit. They extended the run into November. I'm due back in New York the day after tomorrow to begin rehearsals for *Phantom*."

"Super."

"And you? How's the insurance business?"

"Can't complain. Well, I could complain, but then I'd be a

woman." An old joke.

"Speaking of which, where's Lydia?"

"She's at home, still recovering."

"Ah, yes. I forgot. How many is it, now? Three? Four?"

"Number five. A boy. Nathan."

"Jesus."

"Hopefully the last one." He laughs nervously, as if his hopes are tenuous.

He had invited me to his wedding, all those years ago, but I was on tour with *Miss Saigon*. Just as well. I could not have borne to see him wed Lydia Henshaw. He has paid the price for eighteen years.

"When did I see you last?" I ask.

"Five years, I think. You were here for the Stratford Festival."

"Right. My last Hamlet. I'm too old now, of course. I have to play the *old* Kings, leave the princely roles for the younger lads." We have a laugh at our advancing age.

There will be a lull in the conversation that surprises only Raymond. I always knew our lives would diverge. After two decades we no longer have anything in common except the history of our years at Laidlaw. While he writes up term-life policies in a fluorescent-lit office tower, I pour over my reviews in the New York Times. While he retunes the carburetor on his snow-blower, I snooze under the hum of jet engines, somewhere over the Atlantic ocean.

We will sit together through the dinner, make small-talk, make tentative plans to get together in the summer, if my schedule permits. It will not, and we will not. This event will mark the dissolution of our friendship. We will afterward continue to pretend, but we will have no further expectations of each other.

During the evening, I will learn of Gutterball's recent and untimely death. Apparently his pistol discharged as he was cleaning it. That's the official story, anyway. *Thylvethter ith now thinging with the angelth. Thit.*

Even old Gillespie, my fellow tenor, will be there, all red hair and stick legs. Despite—or perhaps in spite of—his illiteracy, he will be a prominent local jazz musician. He will be poor, but happy.

The most notable absence of the evening for me will be Frank Dolan. I will know exactly where he is, and the thought will cheer me. Before I leave town, I will piss on his grave.

A finger jabs me in the side, and the reunion dissolves. I look over

102

at Raymond. He jerks his chin toward the front of the class.

"Are you still with us, Danny?" asks Mrs. Stock.

"Yes, ma'am."

"I wouldn't mind so much your sleeping in my class if the snoring weren't so distracting."

"Sorry, ma'am."

"Perhaps you should go to bed earlier, if you're not getting enough sleep."

"We're teenagers," I say, borrowing from my friend's repertoire. "There's no such thing as enough sleep."

That gets a laugh from everyone but Mrs. Stock.

I spend a few minutes listening to the discussion, but contribute nothing further.

Raymond leans in to me. "Hey, Danny, I'm thinking of getting back together with Lydia Henshaw."

"Five screaming kids and a broken snow-blower. That's your future, Ray. Mark my words."

Chapter 11

"I'm going to cut Chemistry."

Raymond looks at me as if I've suddenly sprouted a purple goiter. "What?"

"Frank's in my class," I say. "I can't go."

"You've never cut a class in your life."

That is true. Dado has a perfect attendance record at Laidlaw. Since his health is superlative, he does not have the occasional luxury of lounging in bed with the flu—unlike Raymond, who is forever catching one thing or another that puts him down for days.

"If you ate a vegetable once in a while you might fend off some of these bugs that go around," Danny has said to his friend.

Mrs. Dunsmore embraces the misguided notion that Raymond is a picky eater. She has never forced him to sit at the dinner table until his plate is clean. She is convinced that if her son goes to bed hungry, he will contract scurvy, or wake up in the morning with a distended belly, abuzz with flies. His eyes will bulge and his lips will crack; he will be unable to do anything other than lie silently and forlornly on a mat in a straw hut, if he does not have something—anything—in his tum-tum. So the asparagus gets scooped into the trash bin and the chocolate ice cream comes out of the freezer. Raymond keeps a stash of cookies under his bed so that he doesn't have to get off his posterior when he is striving for the high score on his Nintendo.

Not a day passes in the Doyle household when one or more of the monkeys does not go to bed with an empty stomach or a sore bottom after sitting on a hard kitchen chair for three hours. Carter, in particular, is wasting away because he refuses to eat anything that is not deep-fried, or basted in ketchup. Mrs. Doyle is a sensible and caring mother who expects her children to eat whatever she prepares for them, whether they like it or not.

"But I *hate* mushrooms!" Carter complains.

"Don't use that word, Carter. You've been warned."

"I don't like mushrooms."

"Well, kid, I don't like cleaning toilets and washing dishes, but I do it."

"Why?" Carter's favourite word.

"Because I have to. Because *someone* has to, and I don't see anyone else offering to help." She passes a fleeting glance toward Mr. Doyle, who misses the point. "We all have to do things we don't like. You eat certain foods because they are good for you. They don't have to taste good. Nowhere in the rulebook does it say you are entitled to eat only the things you like."

"Raymond's house evidently doesn't have a copy of that rulebook," Danny offers.

"I don't need any help from you, Mister Gravy-and-Fries. I know where your lunch bag goes every day."

Danny faces off with his mother. "I've tried to explain to you the specialized dynamics of a high school lunch room, Mother. If I arrive with a paper-bag lunch, I open myself to dangerous attention from the factions. Teenagers understand only one thing: conformity. If they are all eating fries with gravy for lunch, I'm compelled, for reasons of personal security, to do the same. I don't like it any more than you do. I'd be a lot happier if I could munch on some carrot sticks or chomp into a tuna salad sandwich. If only—"

"Cut the crap, Danny. I get enough grief from your brothers."

"I'm not giving you grief," cries Carter, a sensitive boy. "The mushrooms make me gag. I can't help it. I don't like the smell."

Toby encourages his brother to adopt a more open attitude toward his dinner by spearing him in the thigh with his fork.

"Ow!"

"Can it, Carter," says Mr. Doyle. He has a secret stash of Caribbean travel brochures that he sadly leafs through in the bathroom. He will never escape.

"Carter," says Mrs. Doyle, "you will sit there until every mushroom is off your plate. End of story." She knows that it takes months to starve to death. She is patient.

Danny notes that his father, too, has scooped the mushrooms to the edge of his plate. Another detractor of the popular fungus. Peck is the only one, besides Mrs. Doyle and Danny, who has cleaned his plate. He eats with gusto, grateful for mealtimes, when he can finally put something in his mouth that is actually edible. His oral fixation persists. He eats with such fervour, it's sometimes hard to sit at the table with him.

"Jesus, Peck," says Danny. "You're snorting. Close your mouth when you chew. It's disgusting."

"Leave him alone," says Mrs. Doyle. "At least he's eating."

"He's not eating. He's *masticating*."

"What's *masticating?*" asks Toby. "Is that something dirty?" He is thirteen, and just beginning to assemble his adolescent vocabulary of profanities.

Danny steps up to enlighten him. "No. You're thinking of mast —"

"Danny!" The woman of the house does not appreciate frank discussions at the dinner table. When the time comes, she will pass down the ancient set of National Geographic, which will serve to fill in all the blanks a growing boy has about life.

He rephrases. "To masticate is to chew like a goddamned pig."

"Language," says Mr. Doyle. He is permitted to use any word he likes, with the exception of the "f" word. His offspring must adhere to a stricter code.

"I'm not a pig," says Peck.

"You're a good boy, Peck," says Mrs. Doyle. "At least someone appreciates my cooking." She shoots another stabbing look at her husband, who has been caught in the mushroom scandal.

"I have Physics," says Raymond. "I can't cut another physics class or Mister Sutherland will call my mother."

"I'm not asking you to cut. If I catch you cutting another class, *I'll* call your mother."

"Jesus. What do I need a mother for, when I have you?"

"Just be at the meeting place at three," I say. "Don't be late."

"I won't be late."

"I want to talk to you before I go into drama club."

"I won't be late." He'll be late.

Leaving school at the end of the day is never as simple as striding out the front door. Because Frank Dolan is clever and adaptable, my departure route must periodically change. The current route is the most complicated yet, requiring passage through a number of unmarked doorways. I have to keep one step ahead of the predators.

Raymond slouches off to discover the many uses for gravity, while I stride toward the library. As the second bell rings, I tingle with the guilt of my truancy. My first offence. I feel a growing paranoia as I make my way along the corridor, as if my crime is stencilled on my forehead. I expect faculty members to leap out from shadowy doorways and haul me by the elbow to the principal's office, where a red stamp will be ceremoniously pressed onto my file: ABSENT. Student hall monitors will rat me out to the authorities, pointing accusatory fingers. "Hooky! Hooky!" they will shout, raising the alarm. When I duck into the library unmolested, my equilibrium returns. It has been a haven for me over the years. The jocks avoid the library at all cost. And I can dodge the surly librarian with adroit flair.

I grab the first book that comes to hand and settle into my usual study cubicle. I catch my breath and look at the book jacket. *Adventures in Breeding.* I briefly thrill until I realize the cover features a horse. I admit I possess a fulsome lack of interest in all things equestrian. I open the book anyway, check the table of contents, turn to Chapter 4: Maiden Run. Everything else, in my view, will be prologue.

I begin to scan the sentences, but my brain refuses to decode their meaning. The topic is too far out of the scope of my interest to engage me.

"Looking for a hobby?" A voice from the next cubicle.

I look up to see Heidi Borland peering down at me, and I begin to tingle again. "I figure I'll be less conspicuous sleeping here if I have the most boring book ever written in front of me. Maybe the evil librarian will take pity and leave me alone."

"As long as you're quiet, she won't bother you."

"She's had a grudge against me ever since I complained about some of the titles they stock here."

"Are you one of those book-burning fanatics?"

"Of course not. I'm just aware of the influence certain topics can have on children."

"We're not exactly children, are we?"

"Speaking of you and me, no. As for the rest—"

"What topics do you object to?"

"*Abnormal Psychology*, for one."

"I was looking for that, recently. It wasn't on the shelf and the librarian said it wasn't signed out."

"It's under my bed."

"Shouldn't that be where you keep your Playboys?"

"I share my room with a preteen. I can't have porn just laying about. I have responsibilities. Anyway, *Advanced Abnormal Psychology* is a better read."

"Thanks. I'll look for it."

"You'll have to look under my bed."

"I'm beginning to see a trend."

"There are a couple of titles left in that section, but they're mostly harmless. I probably won't take them."

"You're discerning. I like that."

"If you're really interested in an in-depth study of dementia praecox, you can come over to my house sometime and we can go through that chapter."

"I'll wait for the movie, thanks."

"It won't be as good as the book. You should know that."

"Nevertheless."

"Anyway, what are you doing here? Skipping class?"

"Free period."

"Me too."

"You're skipping Chemistry."

"How do you know that?"

She shrugs.

"How much of my schedule have you memorized?"

"Most of it, I suppose."

"Why?"

"In case I ever want to bump into you in the hallway."

"I thought you didn't like me."

"I never said that. I just said that I didn't want to go out with you."

"That doesn't make sense. If you like me, you should want to go out with me."

"I'm afraid I'll be disappointed. It's more gratifying to imagine it. Real life hardly ever lives up to expectations."

"Sometimes life can be surprising."

"I'm surprised to see you here. A perfect record up in smoke."

"You seem to know a lot about me. You must be able to figure out why I skipped."

"Writing a Dear Jane letter to Marion Dalton?"

"Somehow, that's the answer I expected from you, but no."

"I heard you had a little trouble with Vick Peterman."

"I think I'm officially on his *to do* list."

"Well, if it's not Marion-related, you must be trying to avoid Frank Dolan."

"Bingo."

"He gives me the creeps. He sits behind me in Psychology and talks to himself."

"No one else will listen."

"He has a particular fondness for you, I've noticed. What's his beef?"

I shrug. "He's been picking on me since grade school. It's just his nature. I don't think he has anything against me, personally."

"He probably just wants a friend. Have you tried being nice to him?"

"If we became friends, I'd have a hard time getting over the fact that he's spent the past six years beating me up and throwing me into mud puddles and calling me names. Besides, I have all the friends I need."

"Shall I leave, then?"

"I'd rather you didn't. I already consider you a friend."

"How sweet."

Before I have time to prepare myself, she leans over and kisses me on the lips.

Moments later, Dado and Heidi are on the warm wrestling mats in the crawlspace beneath the stage, lying side-by-side. The gymnasium is filled with howling boys playing dodge-ball. Out of sight, boy and girl are joined at the lips, sucking on rapture, filling each other's mouths with spit and love. A nervous hand explores the terrain and is slapped down.

"Don't," says Heidi.

"*To deny a face the touch of a hand / To shun a rose that blooms in the garden / To forsake a bird that sings on the branch / Is to prick at a heart of one's true love.*"

"Your hand wasn't going for my face, loverboy."

He repositions himself on the mat. "Wait. There's more—"

"Listen, just keep your paws where I can see them. Otherwise, the smooching session is over."

"*A kind word from a lady of virtue / will—*"

"Okay, Romeo. Spare me the speech."

Romeo rolls onto his back. His lips have miraculously acquired a layer of Chapstick—an unforeseen bonus. "I knew you'd change your mind."

"About what?"

"About me."

"I haven't changed my mind about anything."

"My lips tell me different."

"More bad grammar. You say you're an honour student?"

"True love calls for poetic license."

"You're trying to impress me with colloquialisms and tired quotes."

"I'm trying to impress upon you my unflagging devotion."

"Now you sound like a dog."

"I'm dogged in my determination to win your love."

"I'm not a carnival game."

"You are a prize to be fought for and won."

"That's a somewhat medieval view."

"I'm an old-fashioned chap."

"I'm an old-fashioned girl. I'm saving myself for marriage."

"It's only a matter of time, for us. Why wait?"

"You're pretty confident."

"You've given me hope."

"All I did was let you kiss me."

"Are you saying you haven't changed your mind about going out with me?"

"Yes."

"Yes, you haven't changed your mind, or yes, you want to go out with me?"

"Yes."

"You're a frustrating girl."

"I'm worth it, though."

"You're a good kisser, anyway."

"Thanks."

"Want to kiss some more?"

"Let's go over our lines. We have a half-hour before drama club."

"I'd rather just kiss."

"You would."

"I have a birthday coming up soon."

"The clock's ticking."

"You're the only one who can spare me the disgrace."

"What about Marion Dalton? You could bring her here. I hear she's not particular."

Will no one let me forget about Marion Dalton?

I project myself into the future. A milestone reunion is at hand, and I am late. I stand in the foyer and look at my watch for the tenth time.

"For God's sake, Marion. Let's go!" There is muttering upstairs. I don't need to hear the words to know they are unkind. "Get the lead out!" I don't remember when I started using such crass jargon.

By the time Marion descends, I am slouched on the living room sofa, counting the ridges in the draperies. I lose count when she arrives.

"I can't go to the reunion looking like this," she says.

I look at her. She has been fat for so long, I can't conjure an image of what she looked like before. She gained the weight during her pregnancy and never lost it. She has been on a diet for eighteen years, an effort that has gained her a further thirty pounds. I am resigned.

"You look great."

"You can go without me. Tell them I'm sick. It's the truth, anyway."

She is wearing the black dress she bought six months ago, with the long-term intention of sizing down in order to fit in it by the time the reunion took place. She has failed to downsize, but has managed to squeeze into the garment, which is a laudable feat in itself. If she moves her arms, the dress will explode.

"I'm not going without you. That's ridiculous. Everyone at the reunion is going to have a few extra pounds. It happens to everyone as they age."

"Not you. You're still the same."

"I have a high metabolism. I can't help it."

"I hate you for that."

"You're still a beautiful woman, Marion." I know that she needs to hear the words, even if they don't quite ring true. I am free to compliment her at great length without fear of intimate repercussions. We have not had relations for over five years. Not with each other, at least. That void in my marriage has been filled by my secretary, Sandra. She is young and kind-hearted, and actually believes that I will one day leave my wife for her. I keep her at bay by reminding her that State Farm employees are not permitted to wed.

"Let's just go, Marion. We don't have to stay if you're not having a good time. Aren't there people you want to see after all these years?"

"I wanted everybody to see *me*. Thin and beautiful. Not like this."

"I think you're overreacting."

"What would you know about it? You weren't the most popular girl in school. You weren't looked up to and admired by everyone in the class of twenty-O-two. You were a fucking geek."

"I was not a geek! Don't ever call me that." There are some insults I cannot abide.

"Vick will be there."

"Whoop-dee-doo. We're back on that subject again."

"He's a city councillor, you know."

"He's a Liberal."

"Don't start with the Liberal business. All I'm saying is—"

"—you should have married Vick."

"Since you put it that way, yes. I've wondered what might have happened." She begins to cry. It's just the booze. I don't take it seriously.

I am no longer interested in cheering her up. "You'd still be fat, and you'd still be drunk. The only difference is you'd have a black eye, too." After this, I expect I will be going to the reunion alone, after all.

"You're a bastard!" She flees upstairs, back to the bottle of Vodka she has stashed in her shoe cupboard.

I arrive at the reunion by bus. I do not own a car. I find the public transit experience tranquil, convenient. If Marion had come, we would have splurged for a taxi. The gymnasium is filled with neck-ties and tacky mauve dresses. There are eight-hundred conversations going on at once. Nickleback is echoing through the chamber at an uncomfortable level.

I immediately spot Vick Peterman. He is surrounded by a clutch of his old crones, shaking hands, accepting congratulatory slaps on the back; the popular city councillor who recently reopened the nude beach on the north shore of Toronto Island. His hair is salt-and-pepper, distinguished, dapper. I have nowhere else to go, so I shuffle toward him. I don't have anything to say to him. Perhaps I will just stand nearby and experience his celebrity, second-hand. As I approach, he squints at me, as if he recognizes my face, but can't quite put a name to it.

His arm comes out. "Vick Peterman," he says, gripping my hand in a powerful paw. He is looking for my name-tag, but I slipped past the reception table without filling one out.

"Danny Doyle," I say, wondering if the name will mean anything to him.

My hand is quickly released and his expression changes. The political smile dissolves into a sneer. "How's Marion?"

I sense that he wants to spit, after saying that name. "She's at home, sick." I am fumbling for words. "She wanted to come, of course. She was looking forward to seeing you again."

"Right. Well, you can give her a message for me."

"Sure."

"Fuck off," he says, "and take that piece of shit husband of yours with you." He turns away from me and resumes a conversation with another former jock.

I leave Vick to his friends and promise myself that I will pass along the message to my loving wife.

As I meander through the room, I recognize several geeks. They are in their element, enjoying their ultimate revenge on the jocks. They wear four-thousand-dollar Armani suits and complementary Rolex watches. They wear twenty-two-year-old blondes on their arms. They are all friendly to me; a few even remember me.

"I drive a Hummer, now," one of the geeks tells me, casually. "Imagine a car that size that only seats four!"

We laugh at the absurdity.

"But the mileage is pretty good. It gets about twenty gallons to the mile."

We laugh again.

"What are you up to these days, Danny?"

"Marion and I have a sod farm, north of the city." If I tell them the truth, that I sell insurance policies for State Farm, I know that the conversation will come to an abrupt halt. No one will ask too many questions about a sod farm.

Every geek will tell me he is in "information technology."

"What is that?" I ask.

"About seventeen million a year," they say. Their revenge is complete.

I spot Gutterball in a corner, standing alone. As I approach, I am blessed with a vast array of white teeth: he smiles. Gone are the dark sunglasses; gone are the knee-hugging jeans; gone are the gleaming gold chains and the fist-full of bulky gold rings. He is wearing a black suit and tie.

"Hi, Gutterball."

"Lordy! No oneth called me that for twenty yearth, Daniel."

We shake hands.

"Where's the posse?"

He shakes his head mournfully. "Gone to God, every latht one of them. Lordy! My new pothy all of God'th children, now." He tells me he is a Baptist Minister. His parish is in Regent Park, a rough neighbourhood. He leads a boy's choir. "You come thing with my boyth, thometime, Daniel. Lordy! Them boyth can really thing."

I promise to take him up on the offer, even though my days as a choir boy are long over.

As I scan the shifting crowd, I spot the ponytail. It is mostly grey, but still thick and lush. I approach my old friend from the rear, touch his shoulder. Raymond breaks off an animated conversation with two ageing rockers and turns to face me. His eyes penetrate me, focus on something six feet behind me. He blinks, looks down at my chest where my name-tag should have been, then refocuses on the blank spot over my shoulder.

"Hey, Danny," he says, tentatively, as if he isn't quite sure if he's got the name right.

"Hello, Ray," I say, confidently. I see it all coming back to him.

"Raymond," he says. There is no reproach in his voice. "Jesus. How've you been?"

"Fine, fine. You know. Just the same. And you?"

"Hey, great. You know."

I know. He is a celebrated record producer. He is nearly as famous as the musical groups he produces. He is an industry titan with the Midas touch, a track record for making chart-topping hits. Every garage band in North America dreams of one day engaging his services: a guaranteed trip to the Grammy podium. Raymond has made that trip himself, a half-dozen times.

"What are you up to these days?" he asks me. The most popular question of the night.

I tell him about the sod farm. He is bewildered, has nothing to say about it. I tell him about Marion, about how sick she is.

"Yeah. The blonde. I think I remember her. I wondered what happened to her. You married her?"

I nod. "We have a son. Daniel Jr."

"Great, man. That's great."

"Thanks to the Young Offender's Act, he'll be out of jail soon."

"Super."

I sense that Raymond is restless. We may have once been the best of friends, shared the most important years of our development together, but we are now worlds apart. He is, he tells me, currently re-mastering a retrospective anthology of Nickleback. And he is bringing up a new band: The Jungians. They are from Japan, and will be the next "big thing." He is only comfortable when he is talking about the recording business.

"What happened to your tin ear?" I ask him, a feeble attempt at levity. I quickly realize that he is mortally insulted. The moment is saved when a woman approaches. I don't recognize her until she takes Raymond's arm and gives him a quick but familiar kiss on the lips.

"Hello, Heidi," I say.

She blinks at me like an owl. "Hello." Her eyes, like Raymond's, flit down to my breast and fail to locate the handy name-tag.

I wish to rewind the clock one hour, make a new entrance, this time with the sticky square affixed to my suit pocket. Philip Mason, it would read. I would be a fictitious geek, and a current "information technology" mogul. I would tell everyone that mine is the *silver* Jaguar, parked in the east lot. I would apologize for my wife's absence, due to an unexpected modelling assignment in Milan. I would shake Vick Peterman's hand and ask him about waterfront development opportunities for a man with a lot of zeros burning a hole in his pocket. Vick will lick his lips and pass over his card, encouraging a meeting, early next week. Gutterball will tell me his church needs a new roof, and I will promise to have a cheque in the mail the next morning. The geeks will embrace me. I know their secret handshake. Raymond and Heidi will be glad to see me.

"You, of all people," they will say, "don't need a name-tag, Philip."

Polite liars.

But Einstein was the only man who knew the secret of time distortion, and he is dead; his secret has gone to the grave.

Alas.

"You remember Danny?" Raymond says to Heidi. "Didn't you two take drama club together?"

Heidi's face softens. "Yes, I do. Of course. Nice to see you, Danny."

"You look really good," I say to her. Weak adjective, lame adverb. Heidi has always put the whammy on me. Anyway, it's true; she is still a beautiful woman. She has finally grown into her features. "Are you and Ray—?" I wave my finger between them.

"Married? Yes. Eighteen years, now." She hugs her rock 'n' roll husband. "He's getting a bit long in the tooth for this thing," she says, tugging lovingly at his ponytail. It must be an old joke between them because Raymond accepts the jibe in stride.

"Danny's married to Marion," Raymond tells his wife. "Remember Marion?"

"No."

"The blonde. Popular, pretty. You remember."

"Sorry."

"Anyway," I say, "she's sick tonight. She sends her love to all."

"Well," says Raymond, "good to see you, man. Take it easy." He turns away from me. They both turn away from me, shut me out, shut me down. I am no longer of their world. I've been left behind, like the grubby hallways of Laidlaw High. I've become an insignificant piece of nostalgia. For my old friends, Raymond and Heidi, the ship sailed a long time ago. I never made it as far as the port.

I have nowhere to go but home.

The bus is crammed with rowdy teenagers. There are no seats left, so I am forced to stand. The teenagers pass sidelong glances at my neck-tie and giggle. "Pay attention, kiddies!" I want to shout. "Take a good look at your future, if you aren't careful." But my opinion no longer matters to anyone. Nobody heeds an insignificant piece of nostalgia. I am resigned.

Chapter 12

When I open my eyes, I am alone in the crawlspace. Heidi is gone.

Blinking at the harsh fluorescent lighting in the corridor, Dado strides purposefully toward a rendezvous. The three o'clock bell signifies the end of another educational day. But the day is not yet done, not by a long shot. Danny Doyle has things to do. And there is one student at Laidlaw who still has a lesson to learn.

Raymond arrives at the meeting place right on time, ten minutes late.

"You're late," Danny says.

"I fell asleep."

"That would have been my first guess."

"I can't help it. Sutherland is such a bore, it's hard to stay awake when he's talking. Physics is the most boring subject on Earth. I don't know why we need to learn all that shit. It's not like I'm ever going to become a physicist. Most of what we learn in school is useless."

Danny sighs. "You're not here to learn mere facts, Ray. You're here to learn how to *learn*. You're never going to graduate if you sleep through your classes. If you don't start paying attention, you're going to be a world-class bus driver." Danny's work is never done, where his friend Raymond is concerned. "Ten years from now, when you're attempting to move a giant rock, you'll be sorry you slept through your lessons on leverage after your back goes out and you lose a week's pay, laid up in bed."

"That's stupid."

"The essence of problem-solving can be applied to anything you do in life. That's what learning is all about. If you haven't mastered the art of problem-solving, you'll never get anywhere. Now, I agree that the current curriculum could use a bit of an overhaul. It's unconscionable to me that they can waste three hours a week teaching us how to cobble together a wooden bird house, when three-quarters of the students can't spell *meretricious*."

"Jesus. Who would want to? Anyway, my mother really liked the bird house I made for her, last year."

"The point is—"

"—here we go again with the point."

"We need to get back to the basics, learn how to read and write, cover the fundamentals of math and science."

"You sound like my father."

"God forbid."

"Anyway, what did you want to talk about? I have to get home."

"I want you to meet me tonight."

"*Survivor's* on. It's the last episode."

"Listen, Ray, I've warned you about watching that sort of dreck. You're better off playing Nintendo."

"I'll probably do some of that, too."

"No, you won't. You're meeting me at eight o'clock."

Raymond gives Dado a suspicious glance. "What's going on? Does this have something to do with Frank?"

"Yes. You don't need the details now. Just be at the ravine at eight."

"It's cold out. I don't want to hang out in the ravine."

"Don't whine. I have to get to drama club. Just be there. And don't be late." Danny reaches for the doorknob, turns back to Raymond. "Bring a shovel."

"A shovel? You've gone completely nuts, Danny."

"Just do it."

The two boys casually exit the storage room, blend into the flow of students making their escape from Laidlaw.

"Eight o'clock!" shouts Danny, as they separate. Raymond waves a hand over his shoulder and disappears into the crowd. Danny watches him go. He is pessimistic about Raymond's prospects for arriving promptly. All is going according to plan.

As I make my way toward the stage, I scan the faces in the hallway without making eye contact with any one of them until I spot

Marion Dalton. I quickly look for a doorway to duck into, but too late.

"Hi, Danny." She waves me over to her locker.

I approach, resigned. I recall the dream, remembering how she looked, two decades older: angry, drunk. Fat. I shudder. Some of her previous luster has gone; or perhaps it is an illusion. Then again, perhaps her previous luster was the illusion. "Hello, Marion."

"Some of us are going to meet at the mall, later. Why don't you come?"

"Sorry. I have a previous engagement. Some other time, maybe." I try to imagine who comprise "us." Half a dozen giggling, lacquered cheerleaders, chewing gum and touching each other's hair. I'd be on safer ground hanging out at the 7-Eleven with the gangbangers. A gunshot wound is a more pleasant way to die.

"You can come by my house, later, if you want." She freezes my toes with an ice-blue look. There is something of Lydia Henshaw's desperation in her eyes that makes her seem pathetic to me.

If only I could remember the words I said to Marion, outside Ms. Wilcox's classroom, I could package them and sell them for a fortune.

"I'm sure I'll be late with this other thing," I say.

"Darn it!"

It takes me a moment to realize she's cursing a faulty lipstick balm, not me. "But some other time, as I've said." I am conflicted. My brain tells me I am doing the right thing by discouraging any further contact with Marion. I know that she is nothing more than a pretty face and a perfectly arranged body. I know that she actually believes that she will one day share a spacious and trendy Manhattan loft with two of her closest friends, even though they will all be coffee shop waitresses. She watches *Friends* reruns religiously. I know that she is not interested in anything that does not directly pertain to her, and her beauty. And that last is the only thing we have in common. Some other part of me, a part not connected to my brain, is fascinated by her. No matter how many times I remind myself that she is a silly, insipid girl, I find it hard to let go of her entirely. I am drawn not so much to her beauty as to the idea that someone so beautiful could be drawn to me. I am, frankly, not her type. I am three inches shorter and considerably less muscular than her type. I lack membership in any acknowledged faction, and manage to keep my preternatural charisma at bay through sheer willpower—or so I thought.

Marion has empowered me in a way that I never thought

possible. She wants *me,* and I am the one in control of the situation. A thousand of my school mates dream of standing where I stand, having a conversation with Marion Dalton, and what separates me from them is that I have the power to deny her what she wants. I like the power, but it's a paradoxical balancing act. If I succeed in rebuffing her, I eliminate my power over her; yet, the longer I stall, the more involved I must become.

I consider taking her to the mats beneath the stage. Then I remember being pressed into the lockers by Vick Peterman, having my skull crushed and my arm bent in an unnatural way. I remember his halitosis and his psychotic jealousy, and I know I am doing the right thing.

"I have to go," I say. "I'll be late for drama club."

"Call me, later," says Marion. She hands me a sheet of paper with her telephone number penned on it. The Grand Prize. Then she kisses me. Again.

I quickly extricate myself and trot away.

Danny is taken by surprise as Frank Dolan suddenly blocks his way. Had he not been distracted by Marion's kiss, he would have expected the meeting. He was, in fact, counting on a confrontation with Frank. If nothing else, Frank Dolan is predictable.

"Hello, Boyle," says Frank. "We missed you in Chemistry."

"Get lost." Danny focuses on Frank's face and realizes that the eyes show no signs of life, as if he is already dead. He wonders if they have always been like that, or if they are harbingers of fate.

Frank is standing uncomfortably close to Danny. "Not very nice, after I did you the favour of telling Mister Sanjit that you were cutting class."

"Don't do me any more favours."

"You're welcome. It was my pleasure." He sneers, looks down on Dado. There is a pause. He appears to have nothing further to say on the matter.

"I'm in a hurry, Frank. If you're going to push me down and kick me, I wonder if you could just get on with it, so I can get to drama."

"What do you take me for, Boyle? Some kind of bully?" He backs Danny into the wall.

"I hate to be brutally honest, but the general consensus seems to be that if you tried to be nice, now and again, you might have better

120

luck finding a friend. I'm telling you out of genuine concern."

"You ought to be more concerned with your own life."

"I think my honesty can help us both have a better life."

"I have all the friends I need, right here." He holds up a fist.

Danny does not need an introduction. "We've met," he says, evenly.

"Say hello, again." Frank Dolan's only friend strikes Danny in the side, just below the ribcage.

Dado's lungs are paralyzed, just long enough for panic to set in. He expels a long, feeble wheeze before breathing resumes.

"How do you like my friend?" he asks.

Danny waits for the oxygen to take effect before answering. "A bit of a one-note act."

The friend reconnects with the same spot beneath Danny's ribcage. "Yeah. He can play the same note over and over again, all day long. But it's a good note, you have to admit. It's a hard note to ignore."

"Agreed," gasps Dado.

"And he's very persuasive."

"True."

Frank helps Danny straighten up. "I'm afraid I have some bad news for you, Boyle. Only queers take drama club. I know your parents will be heartbroken, but you have to tell them the truth. You can't go on living this lie."

"You could take your comedy act on the road. You'll be a smash hit. Anyone who doesn't laugh at your jokes gets a knuckle sandwich."

"I think you're on to something." His hand goes to Danny's throat and begins to squeeze. "Let's hear you laugh."

Dado gurgles pathetically.

"Take it outside, boys," says Coach Fenchurch, passing, sneakers squeaking as he retreats toward the gymnasium, where basketball practice is commencing. He can't be bothered with this incident; he has twenty-four eager victims awaiting his own brand of pain and humiliation.

The hand releases Danny's throat, pins his shoulder to the wall. "Let's take it outside, Boyle, like the coach says. You can sing some *hosannas* for me."

"I'm late for drama."

"This isn't dramatic enough for you? I can dial it up a bit."

"No thanks. After all these years, this is beginning to get boring."

Frank's friend finds Danny's solar plexus. "How's that? Exciting?"

Danny accepts the pain, knowing that he will dole it out, before long. "It's boring, Frank. And so are you. You should have outgrown this bully phase years ago. You have to admit it's pretty childish."

"My parents can't afford a Nintendo, and it's more entertaining than television."

"Some day you're going to pick on the wrong person and wind up dead."

Frank laughs. "Didn't you know, Boyle? I've dropped all the other weasels from my roster. It got to be too much, trying to keep track of them all. I needed to pare down the operation, focus my energies. You're my only client left."

"Like I said, you're going to pick on the wrong person and wind up dead."

"Are *you* going to kill me?"

"What if I am?"

Frank's face lights with mock alarm. "Ooh! Help, help. Call nine-one-one."

"Forewarned is forearmed."

"I only need two arms to take care of you, choir boy."

"You're cracking me up, again."

The solar plexus receives another friendly gesture. "I don't like to be threatened."

"Tit for tat."

"You're a regular cliché dictionary, Boyle."

"You're a cliché bully."

"Then we're a match made in heaven."

"Good one," says Dado, meaning the cliché. "I have a proposition for you."

"Sorry, Hosanna. I'm not queer."

"I'm not so sure about that." Danny's ribcage regrets that last comment.

"You're in a self-destructive mood today."

"I want to finish this, once and for all."

"I'm sure you do, but it's not about what *you* want."

"Tonight. You and me. A final grudge match to end it all."

"You want to fight me? Daddy been giving you secret boxing lessons?"

"Off school property. No witnesses. Just you and me, alone."

"What about your girlfriend Raymond? You'll need someone to call you an ambulance, afterward."

"He's not invited."

"I don't see the point of it. I can beat you up any time I like. Besides, I was planning to watch the final episode of *Survivor*, tonight. Maybe some other time."

"Maybe you're scared."

The hand grips Danny's throat again. "Why wait? Let's go now."

Danny feels the panic welling up again. He needs time to prepare. "Tonight. Eight o'clock, in the ravine," he croaks.

"You're on, Boyle. Better use this time to write your will."

The hand releases Danny's throat, and Frank is gone.

The plan is in motion. There is no turning back.

Chapter 13

I am the last to arrive backstage. Twenty of my fellow thespians are loitering near the rehearsal table. Heidi Borland is among them, radiant in her nascent way. In the vicinity roam an additional ten bodies: set builders, lighting grips, a stage manager, and Mrs. Banks's assistant, Mr. Turcott.

Mr. Turcott desperately wants to direct a play. He wants Mrs. Banks's job, but her tenure stands in the way of his ascension. He was a professional actor before he was forced to fall back on his teaching credentials, and his flame for the stage still burns brightly. Where Mrs. Banks is an academic study of the craft, Mr. Turcott is raw emotion.

"I applied at the Actor's Studio, in New York," he tells me. "But I didn't get in. Instead, I took a role in Grand Bend that summer, and never got back to New York." His eyes turn glassy as he ruminates.

"Well," I say, "at least you went for it, Mister Turcott. Just think how badly you'd feel if you hadn't tried at all. You'd be here, wondering what might have happened, where you'd be today, if only you'd made the effort."

He sniffs. "Of course you're right, Danny. Anyway, I read Stanislavski's book."

"I'm sure you were better off reading the book, instead of getting a third-party interpretation of Stanislavski's method. I hear it's been somewhat corrupted, over the years."

"I've heard that, myself, you know." He is cheering up. Even the faculty need my support. "Still, the Actor's Studio has launched a number of notable careers."

"James Dean," I offer.

"And Marilyn."

"Brando."

"He was good, wasn't he?"

"Yes, sir. The best."

"Eli Wallach, too."

"Sydney Poitier."

"Marvin Nussbaum," says Mr. Turcott, wistfully.

"Who?"

"Oh, just someone I knew, back then."

"I don't know the name. Has he been in something I might have seen?"

Mr. Turcott shakes his head. "I doubt it, unless you've taken an Alaskan cruise, lately."

"You're losing me, sir."

"We were…friends." He sniffs again. "The very best of friends. We did everything together. We both decided to become actors. We took acting classes and joined an amateur theatre group. It was so much fun, I can't begin to tell you. We got our Equity cards on the same day. We waited tables and saved enough money to make the trip to New York. Every actor's dream. Of course, we would have liked to go Juilliard, but that was beyond both our means. We didn't exactly have the full support of our families. C'est la vie. Anyway, we filled out our applications to the Actor's Studio and Marvin was supposed to deliver them to the front office."

"What happened?"

"Somehow, my application got lost on the way."

"What about his?"

"His arrived, all right. He got the audition."

"And you—?"

"Shut out. By the time I filled out a new application and got it to them, the roster for that session was full. Of course, I felt that, after everything we had been through together, Marvin should have backed out. We were a team. We were in this together. Or so I thought. He refused to throw the opportunity away. He claimed he'd make it big for both of us." Mr. Turcott gives me a hard look. "What sort of rationalization is that? He simply put his own selfish needs above our friendship."

"Shameful, sir."

"Anyway, I came back to Canada, alone and devastated. Not that I lacked for work, mind you. I had a good run in Grand Bend, that summer. I'll bring in the reviews, some day."

"And what happened to Marvin?"

"I never saw him again. After finishing at the Actor's Studio, he couldn't get work. He sent me a few postcards, complaining of a New York theatre scene that has no interest in *real talent*. His words, not mine. Eventually, he took a job with Carnival Cruise Lines. He's a one-man lounge act. He sings elevator music to retirees."

"So, there is justice in this world, after all."

"He sabotaged a wonderful relationship so that he could do John Denver covers on the high seas."

"We all have to make difficult decisions in life, sir. We take risks and hope for the best. It doesn't always work out for the best, though."

"No."

"Your loss is our gain, sir." I nimbly pluck him out of the doldrums.

His head rises. "Yes."

"Missus Banks would be lost without you."

"Yes, that's true." An actor's best friend is his ego.

"I'm sure you're happier without Marvin and his selfishness, sir. You don't need friends like that in your life."

"No."

Mr. Turcott resembles a hairless ferret, with obtruding eyes that whisper of potential thyroid problems. He is dangerously thin, a condition directly related to both a nervous condition and bulimia. I once caught him purging in the boy's room, and was sworn to secrecy. I agreed to keep his secret only if I was permitted to lecture him, privately, on the dangers of eating disorders and the benefits of therapy.

"Remember Karen Carpenter," I say. "Cut down at the zenith of her career by anorexia."

"She had a lovely voice."

"She sang like an angel, sir, and now she sings *with* the angels."

"A tragedy."

"She deprived us of a great gift."

"There's got to be a morning after," he says, quietly.

"Self-esteem should always be your number-one priority." Many laymen confuse self-esteem with ego. The two are mutually exclusive. The ego can be a convenient mask behind which we can hide, but self-esteem is our bulwark. You can't fool yourself. "Have you given any further thought to therapy?"

"I can't afford it on a teacher's salary, Danny."

"What price sanity, sir? You'd be able to come to grips with your anger with Marvin."

"I'm not angry!"

"Gather round, people," says Mrs. Banks. "Time is short."

Dado gives Mr. Turcott a look and winks, at which the assistant director shuffles away to supervise the painting of the balcony. Danny takes his usual place across the table from Heidi Borland. He is impatient for real rehearsals to begin, eager to be given full license to act out his love for Juliet.

At the moment, Juliet appears to be ignoring her leading man.

"You disappeared," he whispers, across the table.

Heidi's dark eyes drill a burning hole in his head, then flit away.

"Are you upset about something, Heidi?"

Again, the eyes come, drench Danny in fast-acting poison. When he fails to drop dead, they turn away, again.

"Look," says Danny, "if you're mad—"

"Mad?" hissed Heidi. "Mad? You're the one who must be mad."

"Actually, I'm the one who's confused."

"You're mad and confused. I'm just mad."

"I can see that. What can I do to help?"

"Shut up."

"Is that your suggestion, or just a mad outburst?"

"Take your pick and shut up. I mean it. I don't want to talk to you."

"That's going to be hard, given our present circumstance, Juliet."

"I'll give it a shot, if you will."

"Don't be angry."

"*I will be angry: what hast thou to do?*"

"We've just spent an hour kissing in the crawlspace. Why are you still resisting?"

"*I see a woman may be made a fool, If she had not a spirit to resist.*"

"I think we're in the wrong play, Heidi."

"Go play with yourself. Go play with Marion Dalton."

"You *are* jealous."

"After what you said to me back there, I feel nothing but scorn for you."

"What are you talking about? What did I say to you?"

"Don't play stupid, Danny. At least I know you're not stupid, whatever else you may be."

Dado frets. This is all too familiar. Dog has done it again. He is spoiling everything. "Did I fall asleep in the crawlspace? I do that, sometimes. I'm sorry. Sometimes I talk in my sleep. Was I talking in my sleep?"

"Don't be a fool. You were wide awake."

"Just tell me the part that offended you. If you tell me that, I can prevent it from ever happening again."

"I promise it will never happen again, because I never intend to talk to you again."

"That's a bit drastic, Heidi. It's not fair that you won't tell me what I said that was so awful."

Heidi pauses, measuring her words. "It's not that it was so awful. It's that it was so *true!*"

"For Christ's sake, what did I say?"

It's funny how loud silence can be, at times. This is one of those times. The room is absolutely quiet. Thirty pairs of curious, blinking eyes regard them. Danny doesn't recall when they had stopped whispering. One of the stagehands drops a screwdriver. The stage manager coughs. Danny can hear Heidi's heavy breathing.

Then, from the far end of the table, someone begins to clap. Slowly. Other's join in, until the pair are basking in wild applause. Dado can't suppress a satisfied grin; they are a powerful team.

"Bravo!" shouts Mr. Turcott, clapping madly.

As the ovation subsides, Mrs. Banks says, "Nice work, you two. Heidi, you made good use of those lines from *Shrew*. Good for you."

Danny nods in agreement, but sees that Heidi is not impressed. She can't let go of the anger. Before he can offer congratulations, she rushes away from the table and flees to the dressing room. Mr. Turcott follows her.

Less than a minute later, Mr. Turcott returns, flushed. Danny can imagine what Heidi must have said to him. "She'll be out in a few minutes," he says, unconvincingly. "Miller! Pick up that screwdriver!" He gathers up his set builders and gets them working.

Mrs. Banks rattles her papers. "Okay, people. We can start without Heidi. We'll take it from the top."

As Gregory and Sampson kvetch about the Montagues, Danny

stares at the empty seat across from him and permits his mind to wander.

During my middle-school years, Elliot Manson and I were inseparable. We were a gang of two. We called our gang The Ravine Rebels. We wanted matching leather jackets, onto which we could stitch our emblem; alas, our mothers intervened. Elliot was a year older than I, but failed to measure up to me in size. A congenital hip defect stalled his physical development and, after a second round of corrective surgeries, forced him to repeat the fifth grade. To this day he walks with a discernible swivel, but at least his hip no longer makes strange popping sounds as he walks.

Theoretically, the ravine has always been off-limits to me, and my brothers. Since the monkeys are all susceptible to tales of bogeymen and undercurrents—both of which have, according to legend, whisked off young boys, over the years—they prefer to play in traffic. Rapists and rapids could not deter me; the ravine is my territory, my playground. Because of Elliot's weak hip, we most often descended to the ravine along Pottery Road, which winds down the escarpment at a more comfortable grade. The alternative was a steep path that sloped down from the Laidlaw High School playground.

Unlike Raymond, who is for the most part blithe and optimistic, Elliot was a brooder. Even at twelve he had baggage. His parents were divorced several years earlier, and manage to cling stubbornly to their acrimony to this day, first embittered by love and now poisoned by loneliness. Neither has remarried.

"I'm never getting married," said Elliot. We were on a small jetty, where we often sat for hours, tossing an endless supply of stones into the brown river and talking about the life that was ahead of us.

"Never say never," I said.

"What's the point? It always ends up in the shitter."

"Not always. My parents are happy." I wasn't so sure, though. I couldn't say, with utter confidence, that my parents were happy. At best I could say that they maintained a functioning alliance. If they once knew romance, I have seen no evidence that it still exists between them. Perhaps they are discreet.

"My father's an asshole." Elliot was always quick to judge. He is ruled by his emotions, which are a dark force within him.

"No one is perfect."

He looked at me with a raised eyebrow, then flung a stone at the head of a large rock that lurked just beneath the surface of the water, a dozen yards out. In the spring, the rock is completely submerged. A threat to the hulls of passing boats. By mid-summer its dome is exposed, a menacing shadow, like a crocodile patiently waiting for dinner to drift by. "My father's a perfect asshole."

"You're too hard on him."

"He left us."

"He must have had his reasons."

"He didn't want to be tied down. He didn't want a family, anymore."

"Bullshit. That's your mother speaking. She's infecting you with her own anger. She shouldn't do that."

"She's got it rough. When he does pay up, it's not enough. She never has enough money."

That much was true. Elliot and his mother lived on the verge of poverty in a shabby subsidized high-rise. She worked as a receptionist at a pharmaceutical firm. Over the years, Elliot's bum hip has been a financial burden on the household.

Elliot's stone struck the crocodile rock. He cheered up, momentarily. "That's one for me."

"Nice one." I encouraged him at every opportunity, knowing that I was fighting a losing battle against his gloom.

"I'm going to be a cop when I grow up."

"A noble profession," I said.

"I want to kill people."

"I don't think that's part of the daily life of a cop. I think they mostly give out speeding tickets and pick up drunks off the sidewalk."

"Sometimes they kill people."

"I doubt they enjoy it."

"I would. I could be a professional hit man. That would be cool."

"You ought to figure out which side of the law you want to be on, before you make your final decision."

"The law doesn't mean anything. The law is stupid."

"Sounds like you've made your decision, then."

"You have to be smart to be a hit man. You can't just walk up to somebody and blow them away."

"No."

"You have to be sneaky."

"Right."

"Smart and sneaky. You have to plan how you're going to do it, you know, figure out if you want to make it look like an accident, or a suicide."

I admit my young friend had a dark side that I didn't quite fathom. "You'll feel guilty. You can't kill someone without feeling guilty. You, in particular, need to foster some more positive emotions."

"That's the beauty of being a hit man. You don't have emotions. There is no guilt."

"Listen, Elliot. You want a profession you can be proud of."

"I'd be proud to be a good hit man."

"Just imagine meeting a nice girl. You go over to meet her parents, and her father asks you what you do for a living. What are you going to tell him? That you're a heartless killer? A remorseless assassin? That's not going to go over very well with your new in-laws. Come to think of it, that's not going to go over very well with the girl, either."

"I won't care what they think. Don't you see? No emotions. That's the secret."

"You have plenty of emotions, but they're all related to anger."

"I'm not angry." He threw a smooth stone at a swirling gull and missed. "Shit. Lucky fucker."

"You'd better work on your aim if you're going to be a hit man," I said. I watched the gull swoop overhead, oblivious to the danger we presented. It waited patiently for one of us to die on the jetty, unaware that neither of us tasted like fish. I thumbed the smooth rock in my palm, leaned back, and let it go, into the grey sky. I didn't bother to take aim; my shot was a symbolic gesture, a message to the bird that we weren't quite ready for lunch, yet. Two seconds later, the gull's rhythm was disturbed. It squawked, rolled, recovered its equilibrium.

"Jesus, Danny! You hit the fucker!" Elliot was elated, perhaps a little envious.

"Lucky shot," I said. But I felt lucky only insofar as the bird appeared to be uninjured. At least it took the hint and moved to safer airspace across the river, where the muddy shore was unpopulated. For the next hour I restricted my missiles to the stone crocodile. I got two direct hits and took the lead.

"Look over there," said Elliot. He pointed over my shoulder, to the path along the river bank. "Isn't that Millhouse?"

A hundred yards downstream, Stanley Millhouse meandered slowly in our direction. He was my age, but looked younger. He was a premature birth. He was prey. "What's he doing down here?" The ravine was no place for an underdeveloped lad to play. If the river didn't get him, the bogeymen would.

"He's got a dog," said Elliot.

Indeed, there was a rambunctious dachshund circling him, sniffing every blade of grass and empty soda can, rushing the shoreline, barking at the water. I have never been able to appreciate dogs; their blind devotion cannot make up for unwavering stupidity. Millhouse's wiener dog would never learn that all blades of grass smell pretty much the same, and the river will never be intimidated by its fierce bark.

"I hope he doesn't spot us," I said. Millhouse was a pest. There was no room in the Ravine Rebels for him. As a gang of two, we were complete.

But Elliot had other ideas. "I want to see the dog."

"I don't want Millhouse hanging around us all day."

"Come on. Let's go see his dog." Elliot was deaf to my objections. He rose—awkwardly, thanks to his hip.

We moved toward shore, Elliot limping over the uneven surface of the jetty.

"Let's just leave him alone," I protested.

Elliot was tenacious.

Millhouse ambled slowly. He had not seen us. He was distracted, waving a small stick over the dog's head, driving the animal crazy. It desperately wanted the stick, but with legs better proportioned for a gopher, the dachshund could not jump. I couldn't help feeling that the stick would be just another bitter disappointment for the dog, hardly worth the energy expended to attain it.

We reached the shoreline, closed the distance to Millhouse. Elliot was nearly as excited as the dog. I noticed too late that he still had a rock in his hand. He sent it aloft with an easy flick of his wrist. I watched with growing alarm as it arced beautifully toward Millhouse. Even before it came down, I knew it was a good shot, a lucky shot, like my throw at the gull. The stone glanced off the top of Millhouse's skull and skittered away into the grass. The dog ran after the stone, sniffing, sniffing.

Millhouse fell to his knees and gripped the top of his head. He began to bawl.

"What a shot!" yelled Elliot. "Did you see that? Holy shit!"

I failed to get caught up in Elliot's elation. "I think you hurt him," I said.

"I should score two for that one. That puts me ahead by one."

"We'd better see if he's okay."

By the time we reached Millhouse, he had rolled onto his side. He would not let go of his scalp. The stupid dog was scampering about its master's head, eager to play this new, fun game. It barked madly, poked Millhouse in the ear with its wet nose.

"Are you okay?" I asked, lamely. Even though I did not throw the rock, I was the one who was sorry. As the leader of the Ravine Rebels, I bore the conscience for the entire gang.

"Ow! Aieee!" Millhouse rolled around on the ground, writhing in pain, trying to escape his dog's wet nose.

Elliot was laughing, not at Millhouse but at the nutty dog. "Look at that thing. It's going crazy." He went down on his haunches. "Come here, fella," he cooed, holding out a hand.

The dog ignored the hand, continued to prance around its master's fetal form.

I tried to get closer to Millhouse. "Take your hand away," I said to him. "Let me see your head." As I knelt down, I saw that there was a small amount of blood on his fingers. I suddenly didn't want him to take his hand away. If he saw the blood, he might go into shock. "You'll be fine." Somehow, my words failed to comfort him.

"Come here, boy." Elliot made clucking sounds. He would not rest until the dog responded to him. "Come here, dammit!" He picked up a twig and waved it. The dog noticed the twig, wanted the twig, was nuts for the damned twig, didn't care who was offering it. It lunged desperately for the twig. Elliot stood up, lifting the twig high, out of reach for the nearly-legless dog, satisfied now that he was getting somewhere.

Millhouse stopped bawling, and began to moan pitiably. I helped him sit up. His hand was still stuck to his head. He looked at me with red, puffy slits. His tears were huge.

"You're okay, now," I told him.

He didn't believe me.

Elliot was as frenetic as the dog. He performed an ungainly dance on the grass, waving the stick at the dog. He permitted the dog to get its teeth on the stick, then yanked it away, pulling the dog along with it. I knew that dachshunds, despite their small size and vaguely comical proportions, have powerful jaws that will hold fast to something, if they want it desperately enough. Elliot let the stick go. The dog ran away in victory, but it was short-lived. Elliot found an even better stick, which the dog wanted even more desperately. The game began anew.

"What hit me?" asked Millhouse. At least he could now speak.

Before I could explain the terrible mistake, Elliot spoke up. "It was a meteorite," he said. "Or maybe a bolt from an airliner. They're always losing bolts. The plane's probably going to crash now. Maybe it already has. Hundreds of people are lying dead in a field, somewhere," said my morbid friend, "and it's your fault, Millhouse."

Millhouse began to cry again.

"Jesus, Elliot. Don't say that. I just got him to stop."

"You're lucky you're not dead," Elliot said to the boy. "That bolt could have shot right through your skull and come out your asshole."

Millhouse's wailing escalated.

"It must have been a low-flying airplane. Probably just taking off. Lucky bastard."

"Cut it out, Elliot." When his dark nature got the better of him, I stood up to my friend and tried to rein him in.

The dog was barking with renewed vigour at the better stick. I wondered what it saw. Perhaps it looked like bacon. As Elliot lifted the prize out of reach, the dog broke all previous Olympic jumping records for legless dogs. A gold-medal wiener dog.

"Try to stand up," I said to Millhouse. By encouraging simple motor skills, I could determine the degree of brain damage he might have suffered. I took his elbow and helped him up. He wavered slightly, steadied himself, pushed his thick glasses up his nose, sniffed, regarded Elliot and his loving pooch with something like jealousy. His left hand remained firmly grasped to the top of his bleeding head.

"Come here, Oscar," said Millhouse, feebly. "Come on."

"Oscar?" said Elliot. "You call your wiener dog Oscar?" He laughed.

Even I could not resist a smile.

"Come here, Oscar," Millhouse said. He held out his hand, but without a stick the hand was nothing.

"Oscar, Oscar!" shouted Elliot. "Oscar Mayer! Come on, hot

134

dog!" He began to run, taking the tasty stick with him, the dog in hot pursuit.

"Come on, Elliot," I said. "Let's go."

Elliot ignored me.

"Come here, Oscar," said Millhouse. He, too, was ignored by his best friend.

Round and round the stick went, over Elliot's head. "You want the stick, Oscar? You want it? Okay, you can have it." He threw the stick into the murky Don River.

The dog raced for the shoreline and stopped at the verge. The stick was floating enticingly just a few feet from shore, slowly drifting southward. Soon it would be caught in the current and disappear forever. The dog sensed this inevitability and did not like it. It barked madly, scrabbling its miniature legs on the muddy brink.

"Come on," said Millhouse. He picked up another stick from the ground and waved it for Oscar, but it was a smaller stick. Oscar wanted the big one that was now gaining speed in the water.

"Get the stick," shouted Elliot, encouraging the dog to be brave. "Go get it!"

The dog was daunted by the water.

"Come on, Elliot," I shouted. "I have to get home for lunch." This game was more cruel than I liked.

"Fetch the stick!" said Elliot. "Go get it, boy!"

The dog leaned its nose forward, but it was hopeless; the stick was several yards out, now. As the dog barked, it suddenly lost its foothold on the soft shore and dropped into the river.

"Oscar!" Millhouse finally let go of his head and rushed toward his dog. "Oscar! Come back!"

Oscar could not obey. It was at the mercy of stronger forces, barely able to keep its snout above the surface. It appeared to have lost all interest in the stick, now mainly concerned with staying afloat, and possibly reaching the shore. The river's current had its own will, however.

We three scrambled downstream, following the dog's inexorable progress toward Lake Ontario. Millhouse took the lead, continuing to fruitlessly order his dog to heel. Elliot and I lagged somewhat behind.

"Maybe we should call the police," I said to Elliot.

"What are the cops going to do? Shoot the fucking dog?"

"The fire department can rescue him. We should run up the hill and call the fire department."

"Go ahead. I'm staying here to watch."

"Watch what? Watch the poor dog drown?"

Elliot gave me a look. I knew he wasn't a bad person. He was just angry at his parents, angry with his life. He thought it was only fair that others suffer, too. This was merely a phase that he would outgrow.

"Go ahead," he said. "Call the fire department, if you want."

I scanned the river, in case there was a boat. But there were few boats on the Don River at the best of times. I felt I could not leave. I needed to stay and make sure that Millhouse didn't try to jump into the river to rescue his dog; I knew that I couldn't trust Elliot with that responsibility. The minute I ran for help, he would cajole poor Millhouse into leaping into the frigid water.

The terrain along the riverbank was rough and uneven. We had trouble keeping up with the floating wiener dog, who was becoming a speck as he was carried toward the center of the river. Millhouse forgot about his wounded head, now concerned only with achieving a miracle and retrieving his beloved pet.

Our way was soon impeded by the concrete remains of a former quay. A hundred years ago a lumber mill probably flourished here. Nothing remained now save a ten-foot rise of crumbling cement and timber. I followed Millhouse as we made a precarious climb up the rubble. When we reached the summit, I looked down and saw Elliot waiting below; he could not do the climb without causing himself severe discomfort.

"End of the line," he said to me.

I was about to suggest taking the long way round, when Millhouse called out.

"Where is he?" He was frantic.

I looked out onto the river. There was nothing to see but brown ripples. Oscar was gone. "Maybe he made it to shore," I said. But I didn't believe my own words.

Millhouse needed to believe them. He ran ahead. "Oscar! Oscar!" He scrambled down the far side of the old quay and disappeared from my sight.

"What's happening?" asked Elliot.

"He's gone," I said.

"Who?"

"Both of them."

"This is boring. Let's go for lunch."

Chapter 14

Heidi has returned to the table. She looks like a forlorn lover; her eyes are red and swollen from crying. She is a beautiful, sad sight. Impressively, she has prevailed over her anger and is now prepared to work. When she glances at me, I can see, behind the sadness, that she is bravely restraining her more volatile emotions. Her *id* wants her to rant at me, but her *superego* holds the reins. She may make a Freudian out of me yet.

"It's not a question of memorization, Troy." Mrs. Banks is speaking to our incomprehensible Capulet. "You're giving us the correct words, but you are not giving us the meaning."

"I'm not mumbling," says Troy, defensively. His diction is passable. It is his trailer park twang that subverts the Old English text.

Mrs. Banks readjusts her reading glasses, a mannerism that she engages as a way of releasing her impatience. "I think you're taking my definition of iambic pentameter too literally."

Troy jumps in to prove his flimsy comprehension. "Ten beats per line, with five up-beats and five down-beats. I understand perfectly." Another amateur who can't take notes from the director.

"That's correct. However, you must be careful to put the emphasis on the five *correct* beats. Perhaps you'd care to read the first line of your next passage. And, if you will, please exaggerate the upbeats for us."

Troy clears his throat. "*And* too *soon* marr'd *are* those *so* ear-*ly* made."

Mrs. Banks nods. "Good. Now, you've emphasized *And, soon, are, so* and *ly*. Are you certain those are the beats you want to punctuate?"

Troy isn't getting it. He shrugs. "You tell me," he says, petulantly.

"Well, the fact is—"

138

Dado doesn't need to dissect the dialogue. For him, the emphasis is on *ta*-lent, and Troy has none, so the effort on Mrs. Banks's part is wasted.

As he waits for his next scene, Danny studies Heidi Borland. He remembers kissing her, and it seems like a dream. Less than a hour ago they were locked in a clinch, setting the foundation for their Great Love. Danny briefly touched Heidi's breast: his first bona fide sexual act. The tactile sensation of that soft flesh, nestled beneath a thick cotton shirt, is vivid in his mind. Even the brief pain of having his roaming hand smacked away is a pleasing memory, grateful pain. And then Dog intervened, subverting his progress. Danny wants his memory back, needs to know what happened during those blank minutes. He does not like to take the blame for something he did not do. Of course, strictly speaking, he *did* do it, whatever it was. But he is merely the sword; Dog is the swordsman.

I project myself four years into the future. I am ninety-two days away from attaining a BA in Economics from the University of Toronto. I will graduate with honours. The honour means nothing to me. The moment I am released from this academic bondage, I will fly to New York and enrol in the Actor's Studio, and there will be no Carnival Cruise ship lounges in my future. By taking Economics, I have honoured my father, who has, not surprisingly, become his father's son. He would not pay for my post-secondary education unless I study something useful, something to "fall back on," when my acting career comes to nothing. My father is too old to remember what optimism is. I am resigned. This is merely a four-year detour, and will not keep me from my destiny.

It is Saturday night and I have made plans to spend it with my long-time girlfriend, Heidi. She is a journalism major at Ryerson—my mother's alma mater. Heidi was never as serious about acting as I was. I have repeatedly reminded her over the years that she is squandering her god-given talent on journalism.

"You're a natural actress," I say. "You can't ignore your talent."

"I'm not ignoring it. I'm redirecting it to journalism."

"I don't see how writing obituaries for the Post will make full use of your acting chops."

"Maybe I don't want to act, Danny. Just because you want to do it, doesn't mean I have to."

"It's a waste. That's my point."

"You've wasted four years studying Economics. You're not one to talk."

"I'm fulfilling my father's wishes. You know that. You don't have to throw that in my face. Besides, in three months my emancipation will be complete. Then it's the Big Apple for me."

"Break a leg," says Heidi.

After four years—fourteen-hundred-and-sixty days!—we have not consummated our love. My humiliation as a twenty-two-year-old virgin is complete. Heidi is still playing hard-to-get.

"What are we waiting for?" I ask.

"What's your hurry? You've already missed the deadline. The pressure's off."

"That's what you think."

Heidi sighs. She is tired of this conversation. "I'm just not ready."

"It's not like you're a Mormon."

"I have Mormon values. There's nothing wrong with that. Do you want a girl with no values?"

I ignore the question because I am certain that Heidi will not like my answer. "I have values, too," I say. Perhaps not in league with the Mormons, but still solid. I have had a number of opportunities to release the pressure with some of the less virtuous girls on campus. My enduring virginity speaks to my values. I have been utterly faithful to Heidi in the face of overwhelming temptation.

"To be honest," says Heidi, "I'm worried about our future."

"The cold war is over, darling." My attempt at levity gains me a sneer.

"Don't be flippant. I'm trying to have a serious discussion."

I shrug, surrender to the serious issues.

"What's going to happen in three months, Danny? Tell me that."

"We'll be free."

"No. You'll be going to New York and I'll be staying here."

"I want you to come with me."

"I'm sure you do, but that's not going to happen."

"The beauty of journalism is that you can work anywhere."

"I don't want to work in New York. It's unlikely I'd even be able to get a job there. If I'm lucky, I may get a job reporting lost cats in Chilliwack. If I go to New York, I'll wind up being a waitress."

"At least we'd be together. Love is all about making sacrifices."

"Why should I be the one to make the sacrifice? You could get a job in business while I build my journalism career. After I'm established, we can go to New York."

"My artistic temperament won't permit me to work in business."

"You're about to graduate from business school with honours. I think you can handle it."

"I'm an actor," I say, decisively.

"Maybe you will be, one day, but for now you're a business grad. You haven't even been onstage since high school."

"I've been busy."

"You're not being realistic. You think you're going to go down to New York and suddenly become a movie star overnight."

"I'm not selling out to Hollywood. I'm going to *own* Broadway."

"Even if the Actor's Studio lets you in, it takes years to make it."

"I have the stamina."

"I'm sure you do, but what does that mean to our relationship?"

"We stick it out, stay together, no matter the cost. Once I've made it big, we'll be set for life."

"I'm afraid I don't share your optimism, Danny."

"I've made note of that."

"I don't want to get involved in something that's just going to fall apart. We're both bound to get hurt. What if I become pregnant?"

"This is the twenty-first century, darling. Unless you're a Mormon, there are plenty of options for contraception."

"They're not completely reliable. What if there's an accident?"

"Well, there are ways to deal with that, too. Modern medicine has made our lives very convenient."

"You seem to have it all figured out."

"You bet."

"*I'll* go on the pill."

"Sure. Okay."

"*I'll* get the abortion, if I happen to get pregnant. *I'll* put my career on hold, just so I can follow you around the continent, waiting patiently for you to become a big star, even though we'd have better odds with a lottery ticket."

"I think you're overreacting, Heidi."

"Really? Tell me that's not how you'd like to see things go."

"Look, I just want to make love to you. I love you, and I want to express that love in the deepest way possible. It doesn't have to relate to New York or our careers."

"You haven't been listening to anything I've said. I don't want to start something that we aren't going to finish."

"Love is always a risk. No one ever knows if it will last. And even if it doesn't, it's worth it in the end."

"You don't know anything about it. You read that in a book."

"That doesn't make it any less true."

"No, but it makes you that much less convincing."

"True Love will find a way."

"Now you're quoting song lyrics. Jesus."

"I want you to marry me, Heidi."

I have finally surprised her.

"You're crazy."

"I've looked into that. I'm not crazy."

"We can't get married."

"Why not?"

"If only I had a tape recorder, I could replay the last five minutes of our conversation."

"I thought you loved me." She had never said the words, as such, but four years together means something.

"I'm a realist, Danny. You're a dreamer."

"I seem like a dreamer because I believe in myself. I have self-esteem."

"You have an ego the size of New York."

That hurts me. Not because it's not true but because she meant it as an insult. "Let's say, for the moment, that that's true. I have an ego and healthy self-esteem. So do you. That's what attracted me to you in the first place. The only thing I have that you are missing is *passion*."

"I won't deny that. Passion is a symptom of lingering adolescence."

"That's a pretty cynical outlook. All successful artists thrive on passion. That's what moves them forward as artists."

"I'm not an artist. I'm a journalist. Frankly, an ounce of cynicism will serve me better than a truckload of passion."

"Have you forgotten so soon Juliet's grand passion for Romeo? She was willing to cross the Styx to follow her lover. She couldn't bear to live without him. You proved beyond a doubt that you had that passion within you. You can't fake that kind of passion."

"Yes, I can. It's called acting. I was acting, Danny. And let's not forget that Juliet is a fictional character. Her passion is derived from the mind of a passionate *male* writer. If Juliet had been a real woman, she would have thought Romeo a perfect fool for all his romantic buffoonery. After she discovered him supposedly dead, she would have tidied up the room a bit, and then called the authorities. When he woke up, a few minutes later, she would have railed at him for giving her so much emotional strife, and then dumped him."

"I think you've just spoiled Shakespeare for me."

"Welcome to the real world, buddy."

We share an uncomfortable silence.

"Does this mean you won't marry me?"

"*My grave is like to be my wedding bed,*" she says. Heidi leaves the room, slams her bedroom door. I've had my answer.

"—*I will withdraw but this intrusion shall / Now seeming sweet convert to bitter gall.*"

Silence.

"—*Now seeming sweet convert to bitter gall.*"

More silence.

"Danny?" says Mrs. Banks.

"Hm?" Dado rouses himself from the funk of passionless speculation.

"You're up."

He's missed his cue. "Sorry."

Nathan Carter huffs. He is perfectly suited to Tybalt's troublesome character. "I suppose I have to say the line for a *third* time."

"If you wouldn't mind," says Mrs. Banks.

Tybalt says his piece and exits.

Romeo looks deep into Juliet's dark eyes, and is blinded by the light of love. "*If I profane with my unworthiest hand / This holy shrine, the gentle fine is this: / My lips, two blushing pilgrims, ready stand / To smooth that rough touch with a tender kiss.*"

Unprecedented passion sparks in the girl's eyes, illuminates the room. "*Good pilgrim, you do wrong your hand too much, / Which mannerly devotion shows in this, / For saints have hands that pilgrims' hands do touch, / And palm to palm is holy palmers' kiss.*"

The play unfolds, ends in splendid death.

At five-thirty, the club begins to disperse. Heidi gathers up her satchel and beetles toward the exit. I catch up to her in the corridor, grab her by the arm.

She wheels around and growls, "Let go of me!"

I know that I will not have her attention for long, so I get straight to the point. "I'm sorry. I'm truly sorry if I said something to upset you. If there's anything I can do to make it up to you, just tell me what it is."

"Go stick your head in a vice." She turns away and leaves me behind, clipping her heels in a brisk manner that dares me to follow and suffer the consequences.

I don't dare. I have lost her, but I am not resigned.

After gathering my things at my locker, I make my way to an unmarked door in the west wing. Behind the door is a small room, not much bigger than a broom closet. Along the length of the wall to the right, grey metal boxes house the telephone and intercom circuitry, and other mysterious workings of an electrical nature. The room hums ominously. Along the left wall sit small cardboard boxes, and several spools of unused wiring. There is, inexplicably, a large calendar pinned to the wall, detailing the year 1986. There are messy notations scrawled onto the calendar in different inks and leads, and in different variations of handwriting. The notations do not seem to relate to the calendar, or the dates under which they are written; rather, they seem to be temporary tidbits jotted down by electricians who have serviced the grey boxes over the years. The calendar is a giant notepad.

Beyond the last metal electrical box is another blank door. Unless one enters the closet completely, it is easy to miss the presence of this door. It is the most important and useful door I have discovered over the years of my exploration of Laidlaw High, because it leads the way to my safest escape route from the school. I pass through the door and descend a staircase.

The narrow basement corridor is poorly lit. The staff who use the passageway have been lax, ignoring the dark or flickering fluorescent tubes in the ceiling. I move quickly to the end of the corridor, where three doors stand. Two of the doors, I know, are locked. There are some places in Laidlaw where even the most accomplished snoop cannot gain entry. The third door is unlocked. As I reach for the door, I hear a sound at the far end of the corridor. I don't look back; I need to believe it is merely one of the anonymous faces who maintain the school property, shuffling through the hallways like sullen grey ghosts. I leave the sound behind and ascend the staircase. At the top of the steps there is darkness. Another dead light bulb. Recent budget cutbacks have made the service sector lazy, negligent. The unionized workforce has been abused until there is no longer any pride in a job well done. Now an innocent chameleon must suffer for it. I grip the handrail as I go up. I know the way well enough that I do not falter. At the landing, I reach my hand out and easily find the push-bar on the exterior door.

As the door begins to open, a cold February draft shimmies in. Faint shadows appear; because of the winter hours, the sun has already set. Halfway open, the door strikes something solid and stops. I hear an annoyed grunt, some unintelligible muttering. A shaft of fear spikes through my spine. I freeze, wonder if I should turn and flee back down the staircase. Given how my day has gone so far, the possibilities of who might be waiting for me on the other side of the door are worrying. If it's Frank Dolan, I might try to outrun him, but I cannot fully rely on my instinctive will to survive to overcome his superior physical condition. If Vick Peterman sits in wait, he will no doubt have half the football team with him. I will be a human hacky sack, toyed with, tortured slowly. If I am busted by the faculty for entering forbidden areas of school property, I will no longer be safe in school.

When I remember that the outer door will lock as soon as it is closed, my choice becomes clear. I firm my grip on the bar and pull hard. But someone outside has hold of the door's edge. A supremely ugly visage suddenly peers round the door, a hobgoblin with blotchy skin and a gnarly tangle of hair.

I let go of the door. My heart is racing, pounding blood through my ears.

"What's up, man?" says the hobgoblin.

Recognition sets in. I have seen the shaggy brute in the hallways. An eleventh-grade rocker. He pulls the door open and two more hideous faces appear, slit-eyed, grinning mildly. The smell of pot wafts over me. I recover my wits.

"Hey, boys," I say, casually.

"Hey, yourself," says one of the others. He giggles. The third boy giggles in response.

"Where you coming from, man?" asks the first hobgoblin.

"School."

The others redouble their giggling. I must remember this scene, recount it to Raymond in grotesque detail, a warning about the lasting effects of drugs on the human brain. I step outside, and the three boys gaze with childish wonder into the darkness I have emerged from.

"It's a shortcut to the principal's office," I say.

The hobgoblin quickly releases the door and it closes behind me with a *clank*.

"Shit, man. That sucks." They all giggle.

"Take it easy, boys," I say, moving away from them.

"Later, dude," one of them mutters.

Dado inches along the wall. When he reaches the end, he looks around the corner. A trio of skaters is loitering at the far end of the tarmac, comparing injuries. There is no one else. He looks straight ahead toward his destination: the ravine. He must safely cross the soccer field before he can make his way down the path to the valley. This crossing will be his biggest risk; he will be completely exposed for the minute it will take to cover the distance. He licks his lips and readjusts his knapsack, steps out into the open with an even stride. Partially frozen mud crunches under his feet. There is still colour to the sky, a clear night with a waxing moon that illuminates the field and bordering tree-line dimly.

The scenario brings to Danny's mind his first encounter with Frank Dolan. That was not long after Oscar Mayer, the ebullient wiener dog, went to a watery grave in the Don River. As now, it was dusk. Danny and Elliot had separated moments earlier, Elliot headed for the kinder slope of Pottery Road while Danny, late for dinner, ascended the steep path. Near the top of the path, the trees thickened, swayed in a brisk October wind. Even for an eleven-year-old it was a tiring business, climbing the escarpment. Danny was breathing heavily when a shadow seemed to be moving in front of him, coming down toward him. He stopped.

The shadow spoke. "Bears can't run downhill," it said.

Danny squinted at the shadow: a boy, somewhat larger than he, with an indiscernible face. "What?"

"Bears can't run downhill."

"So what?"

"So, if a bear is chasing you, run downhill and it won't be able to catch you."

"I'll remember that, next time I run into a bear."

The shadow took two steps closer to Danny, gaining some features. A broad, flat face with small eyes set too far apart, thick, glistening lips, tiny scalloped ears, sandy hair that appeared to have been slept on recently.

"I'm a bear," said the boy.

"What?"

"I said, I'm a bear."

"You're a jerk," he said. After spending the day with Elliot, Danny assumed a measure of his friend's innate bravado. This being his first encounter with a bully, he had no reference point to regulate his behaviour. Danny hadn't yet learned how to deal with such boys.

"If I were you," said the bear, "I would start running downhill."

Stupidly, Danny was defiant. "If I were you, I'd throw myself in the river."

The bear took the insult in stride. "I'm a generous bear. I'm giving you fair warning. Most bears would just rip your head off without giving you a chance to run away."

"I'm going this way," said Danny, pointing to the crest that was just a few yards above.

The bear shook his head slowly. "That's where you're wrong. You're going down."

With unexpected dispatch, two hands came up and pushed Danny's chest, sending him backward. Because of the steep grade, his feet went easily out from under him. His shoulders and head struck the ground hard, the momentum rolling him over and over. Down he spiralled. One of his legs struck the base of a tree, prompting a yelp, but there was no time to think about the pain. He was rolling down the slope, freewheeling wildly. Fallen branches and stones imbedded in the dirt path scratched his face and hands. He was powerless against gravity. Down, down he went, until he rolled away from the path and landed in a prickly shrub.

Everything stopped. The Earth stopped spinning. The busy traffic on nearby Broadview came to a halt. Even the river below stood still. Danny lay imbedded in the shrub, unwilling to move. He closed his eyes and wished for a deep sleep that would take him away from the pain. If only he could lose consciousness, he wouldn't have to cope. But sleep was out of his reach. And now his ears were detecting a solitary sound: the unmistakable sound of an approaching bear.

"Have a nice trip?" asked the bear.

"No," said Danny, truthfully.

"But I proved my point, didn't I? I mean, there's no way I could have caught up with you if you hadn't rolled into this bush. Tough luck for you. You've just had your leg gnawed off by a hungry bear."

At the moment, Dado's leg was especially pained; he might have welcomed a hungry bear's merciful chomp. "I think my leg's broken," he groaned.

"Well," said the bear, "in that case, the only chance you have is to play dead. Although I admit that practice is debatable. But go ahead and try. Give it a shot. You've got nothing to lose."

Danny passed out.

The cold woke me up. When I opened my eyes, the bear was gone and the sky was black. The autumnal wind rushing up from the valley was picking up, buffeting against my back. I was still entwined in the shrub, lying on my side, facing uphill. It was difficult to separate the cold from the pain. I tried to move, and groaned instead. I managed to pull myself out of the shrub; I was lying face-down on the dirty path. The summit was now as far away as the valley floor. I had to choose which direction I would attempt to go. The pain in my left leg suggested that either direction would be difficult. Instinct told me to go up, a more direct route toward home.

I dragged my hurt leg, grappling for a hold on thick roots and tree trunks to pull myself upward. As I finally lay on the ridge, regaining my strength, I wondered if my absence from home had been noticed, if the authorities had been called, if there were now search parties combing the neighbourhood, calling my name, poking at bushes with sticks. Not far from where I lay, I spotted an old field hockey stick, splintered and abandoned. I used it as a makeshift crutch and got unsteadily to my feet. Blood coursed into my sore leg, causing the ankle to throb. I hobbled across the soccer field. I was still more than two years away from attending Laidlaw, but I was familiar with the grounds, which Elliot and I played in.

As I passed close to the school building, a voice called out from the shadows of one of the west exits. "You okay?"

I stopped, looked into the shadows, could make out a faint form. The man stepped forward, into the moonlight. An old man in a janitor's grey uniform. He gripped the stub of a cigarette in his hand. I didn't like the look of him. To my young and bleary eyes he looked the embodiment of every rapist or serial killer my mother had warned me about.

"I'm fine," I said. I promptly collapsed.

My next memory was of sitting in the passenger seat of a strange car. The old killer was sitting in the driver's seat. He was talking to me, but his words floated around my head without penetrating.

"Are you going to kill me?" I asked, finally. If he was about to confirm my mother's greatest fear, I would be too weak to do anything to prevent it; still, I wanted to know.

"I'm going to drive you home, if you tell me where to go."

"Oh." I told him.

My loving and grateful mother thanked the old janitor for his kind act of mercy, then, once the door was closed on the geezer, turned her wrath upon me. Not only was I an hour late for dinner, I had been playing in the ravine, and managed to get myself accosted and hurt in the process.

"It was just some kid," I protested. "It wasn't a serial killer." I was laid out on the sofa. My mother was inspecting the damage. After producing six children, she was as good as any triage nurse at determining if a trip to the emergency ward was warranted. I still clung possessively to my crutch, waving it in the general direction of the five nosy monkeys who hovered, enjoying the scene. They were thrilled to see the Great Dado receiving reprimand, for a change.

"Put that dirty old thing down," said my mother, "before you take someone's eye out."

"If they lose an eye, it will be their own fault."

"For Christ's sake," my father muttered, from his recliner. He demonstrated his concern for me by staying out of my mother's way.

"There's a nasty bruise on your shin, and your ankle's swelling up. It's a pretty bad sprain. But nothing is broken. That lump on your head serves you right. I'm sure we won't notice the brain damage. You're lucky, buster. It could have been a lot worse."

That last remark was her own subtle way of implying all of the gruesome methods of unnatural death and dismemberment that she had been forecasting, direly and tirelessly, for years. I am certain there was meant to be a lesson in there somewhere. I ignored it. I was the victim of a random act of violence that could have taken place anywhere, at any time.

"You can use one of Carter's crutches until your ankle feels better."

"Hey!" said Carter. "He can't have my crutch." He was always a possessive kid.

"For Christ's sake," said my father.

It turned out Carter's crutch was too small for me, so I continued to limp around with the field hockey stick, wielding it at the monkeys if they wrestled too close to their convalescing elder.

Two days later I was back at school. I met Elliot outside the school doors, as usual.

"What happened to you?"

"I was mauled by a bear."

"Jesus. I didn't know there were bears in the ravine."

"Just remember to run downhill."

Later that day, Frank Dolan introduced himself to me—sort of. I was still using the field-hockey stick to get around, having wrapped the splintered end with two rolls of electrical tape to soften the point and provide better grip on the slick school floor tiles. As I was hobbling down a flight of stairs, the stick was suddenly kicked out from under me. My right hand was firmly gripping the handrail, so I didn't fall.

"Have a nice trip?"

I turned around and recognized the bear, who wasn't a bear at all, but a boy. A boy who was, even then, two inches taller than me. I had him mistakenly pegged as an eighth-grader who might have been held back a grade, at least once. I was surprised later to learn he was, like me, in the seventh grade. By scholastic standards, he was defined as a good student. Some of us might wish to broaden the definition to include the basic social graces.

"Fuck off," I said. Back then, all profanities were still rich and satisfying in their many uses.

"Hey, man," said Frank, putting on a hurt face. "Sorry about the other night." His apology seemed genuine. "How's the leg?"

"Sprained."

"That's tough."

"No thanks to you."

"It could have been worse. It could have been broken."

"Lucky me."

150

"Of course, that's what I was hoping for, but it's always hard to predict how a kid's going to roll."

"You're an asshole. Stay away from me."

Frank smiled, menacingly. "Sure, kid. No problem." He snatched the crutch from my hand and trotted away, laughing.

That was the beginning, thinks Dado, stepping toward the ridge at an even pace, and this is the end.

Chapter 15

Danny lingers at the bottom of the steep path, a little breathless, and inspects the terrain. He knows the general landscape—the ravine has been his playground for most of his life—but now he looks more closely at the details. After a few minutes, he checks his watch in the dim light; he must hurry to McVeigh's, collect Peck from his play date. Before he makes off, he removes from his satchel a coil of thick wire that he has purloined from the school's electrical closet. He drops the coil behind a tree, just off the path, and leaves the scene.

"What took you so long?" says Peck, as McVeigh's front door closes on our backs. We are both laden with the random items that Peck requires to get through his day: a canvas lunchbox; a plastic thermos that only my mother has the dexterity to cram into the box, and which is afterward carried loose; one woollen mitten; two inexplicable abstract watercolours from art class; three Hotwheels; a gorilla mask; a scarf that Peck refuses to wear because it is yellow.

"I'm not late," I say.

"It seems like you're late."

"I'm right on time. Weren't you having a good time?"

"No."

"Why not?"

"I don't like Alex."

"Why do you go there, then?"

"Mom makes me."

"Tell her you don't like him." He doesn't answer. When I look down, he's not there. He has fallen behind. He's kneeling down, picking at something frozen onto the sidewalk. "Come on. Don't pick at that. What is it?"

"I don't know."

"Whatever it is, it's dirty. Leave it."

"Wait." He picks some more.

"I'm not going to wait for you, Peck."

"Go ahead."

"Better yet, I'm going to pound you, and then leave you behind."

"Just a minute." With Peck, threats are hit-and-miss. "I think it's gum."

"For Christ's sake. Don't touch it. You'll get bubonic plague, touching someone else's old gum."

"What's that?" He is still picking at the gum.

"It's where your hair turns blue and your dick falls off."

That works. Peck straightens up, runs to catch up. Since he sits down to pee, he is not worried about his dick falling off, but the blue hair frightens him.

"Put your scarf on," I say. I can see that he is shivering.

"I don't like it."

"You're cold."

"I don't care."

"What's wrong with the scarf? Everyone wears a scarf in winter. I'm wearing a scarf."

"I don't like it."

"*Why* don't you like it?"

"It's yellow."

"So what?" We've been through this before.

"I don't like yellow."

"Why not?"

"I just don't."

"That's not an answer."

"Yes, it is."

"It's not a good enough answer. Tell me why you don't like yellow? Because it's a girl's colour?"

Peck looks up at me. "It's a girl's colour?"

An error on my part. I've just given him another reason to dislike yellow, besides the mysterious reason that he stubbornly refuses to divulge. "Lots of boys wear yellow, too," I say. "Have you seen Raymond's new jacket? It's so yellow, it practically glows in the dark. And Dad wears that yellow tie all the time. Remember that?"

He is not convinced. "I'm not cold."

Even in the dark I can see that his lips are turning blue. "Aren't your hands cold? Where's your other mitten?"

"Gone."

"I can see that it's gone. Where did it go to?"

"Neville took it."

"The bully?"

Peck nods.

"He's still bothering you?"

He nods again.

"Did you look at him, like I told you?"

"He hit me and told me to stop looking at him."

"You have to do it right, otherwise it doesn't work."

"I don't know how to do it right."

"It takes practice. You have to work at it."

"He took my mitten and told me it was a looking fee."

"A looking fee?"

"He said every time I looked at him it would cost me something. He already took my snack money this morning, so he took my mitten instead."

"Well, you should put the one mitten on, at least. You might as well have one warm hand."

He ignores my advice. I know that the lack of symmetry doesn't sit well with Peck. His little brain is crammed with irrational fears and juvenile notions that I can't begin to touch. It worries me, though: this Neville situation. Once I've taken care of my own bully problem, I will have to come to Peck's aid. For the long term, perhaps I can entreat my stingy parents to enrol him in a karate class, so that he might deal with his own future problems more directly. I won't be around forever to take care of him.

"Will you help me fix my model, tonight?" asks Peck. He is an avid, if incompetent, model builder. His preference is wartime airplanes. He uses either too much or too little glue, and he manages to apply every sticker to the assembled aircraft crookedly. And, once completed, there is always an ongoing schedule of maintenance required, since Peck leaves his models lying around on the floor, where he or I will invariably step on them. His work is never done.

"I can't. I have to go out, after dinner."

"Can I come?"

"No."

154

"Why not?"

"It's big kid stuff." A regular phrase of mine, encompassing all the mysteries that await Peck in the distant, unfathomable future.

At home the pecking order is reaffirmed.

"You're late," says my mother, as we enter the kitchen, where the Doyle clan is already assembled for dinner.

The comment is directed at me because I am the eldest, and therefore held ultimately responsible. "We're not late," I say.

"Dinner's been on the table for ten minutes."

"I had to pick up Peck from McVeigh's."

"I don't want to hear any excuses, Danny. I've been listening to excuses all day long."

"He was late picking me up," say Peck.

"I was not." I pinch his arm. Peck responds with a squeal.

"Can it, Peck," says my father. His mind is no doubt working out a fantasy in which he is flanked by a mile-long stretch of white beach, not another human being in sight. The squeals penetrate his filters, upset the credibility of the fantasy.

"If you didn't stop to pick at every piece of gum on the sidewalk, we might have got here sooner."

"Peck!" says Mother. "Don't pick at gum!"

Peck sticks his tongue out at me, his only remaining resource.

We are having meatloaf for dinner. It's Monday. My mother is capable of assembling a decent meal, but only, it seems, for special company. For us it is meatloaf, or any other bland entrée that can be made in bulk. The meatloaf has mushrooms in it, so there is endless complaining from Carter. My father is more astute; he is eating them, despite an aversion. He is resigned.

"I hope you haven't forgotten that you're watching the boys tonight, Danny," says my mother.

It suddenly gets very hot in the kitchen. "I can't. I have to go out tonight."

I get the evil eye. "I told you about this last week. Your father and I have a function. Have you been reading your notes?"

"Yes," I lie, "but I have plans. I can't change them."

"Perhaps we should just cancel our plans to accommodate you," she says, with an overdose of sarcasm.

"For Christ's sake. They're old enough to look after themselves." I've tried that line before, to no avail. Even Lem, who is sixteen, is an irresponsible oaf, more likely than any of the others to set the house ablaze. I am well aware that I am the only one to be trusted in my parents' absence.

"Language," says my father, flatly.

"We don't need him to look after us," says Lem. He isn't offended by the implication that he is not mature enough to take care of himself or his brothers. He wants me to go so that he is free to smoke cigarettes in the basement laundry room. He took up the foul habit a year ago and has managed, unbelievably, to keep it from our parents. He knows that I will not only prevent him from smoking, but will lecture him about its ill effects without respite.

I choose, in this instance, to agree with Lem. "Lem can look after the boys. It's too late for me to change my plans now."

"What's so important that you can't change it?" My mother is a shrewd woman. After nearly three decades of marriage to my father, she has heard it all before.

I am not my father. I am an actor—a future actor, and the simplest definition of an actor is this: a professional liar. My father wears his lies like brilliant tattoos. He can never get past my mother's shrewdness. I, on the other hand, am utterly believable. "I have a script meeting tonight for the play."

"You're not opening for another two months. I'm sure you can reschedule your meeting for some other night."

I am ready for her. "Juliet's availability is a problem. She works part-time in a nursing home." I concoct this element for its sympathy value. "This is the only night she has free this week. We need to have this meeting before rehearsals start."

"That's not my problem, Danny. This was on your list last week."

I give up. Some arguments are not worth having. I will simply wait until they leave, and then go out anyway.

Dado did not want to be a chameleon. It was a necessity borne of base survival instinct. Before his first encounter with Frank Dolan, Danny was amassing a small but growing group of acolytes: kids who looked up to him for advice and guidance, who admired his staunchly conservative politics and aspired to follow his lead down the straight-and-narrow. If not for circumstances beyond his influence, he might have been popular. If Frank had not forced him into exile as a chameleon, he might have *earned* the right to kiss Marion Dalton in the Laidlaw hallways. He would not only be student body president, but also class valedictorian. He would be Prom King, with Marion at his side as his Queen. They would dance the spotlight dance, spin elegantly across the hardwood floor of the gymnasium, evoke tears of joy and envy. A chance encounter with a bear changed all that. An unexpected downhill tumble bounced Danny off the track to popularity. For that reason alone he cannot forgive Frank.

I project myself two hours into the future. The February air is crisp but not cold. I stand on the tip of the jetty and feel the winter air come off the river and envelop me. I am calm. Low clouds have moved in, reflecting the light from the city, softening the shadows in the ravine. My eyes are adjusting to the night. The river, too, is calm, lethargic in this season of hibernation. In two months' time it will once again be a roiling force, ready to take unwary boys to their doom.

At three minutes past eight I hear footsteps crunching behind me. I don't need to look. I know who it is. "You're late," I say, out of habit. I almost call him Ray.

"Your mommy let you come out to play, after all," says Frank.

I turn to look at him. He stands on the shore. If his eyes have not adjusted to the darkness, the jetty will seem to him daunting, a treacherous and unfamiliar surface, possibly booby-trapped. He is being careful. But I have set no traps for him. If he falls into the river, it will be through his own miscalculation.

I take several steps toward him, easily traversing the uneven surface. I am confident in my footing; we are on my turf. I want to unnerve him with my confidence. In a fair fight, on even ground, I wouldn't have a prayer against Frank. This will not be a fair fight.

He is ten paces away, and I can just make out his face. It is the same blank void it has always been. There is no hint of conscience lurking behind those small eyes. If we were at war, I would want him fighting on my side. He is cunning and ruthless. Given a weapon and an enemy, he would be a formidable killing machine.

"Sorry to make you miss the final episode of *Survivor,* Frank," I say, evenly.

"Let's cut the chit-chat, Boyle. You might as well come a little closer, so I can start hitting you."

"You're presumptuous."

"Look around. You've got nowhere to run. You've trapped yourself out on those rocks. If I have to come out there to get you, I'll be forced to beat on you twice as hard."

I do not move.

Frank shifts impatiently. "Hey, you called the fight, Boyle. Let's go, before the sun comes up."

"Maybe we should try being friends," I say. I would never forgive myself if I didn't at least make the attempt.

"Ha! There it is."

"What's that?"

"The begging. I haven't even touched you, and you're already begging for mercy."

"I don't want your mercy. I'm just giving you a final opportunity to do the right thing. To be honest, I wasn't optimistic."

"You're smart not to be optimistic, since you're moments away from a trip to the hospital."

"I doubt it."

"Is your little friend hiding in the bushes with a fist full of rocks?"

"We're alone, but you won't touch me."

"Who's going to stop me? You?"

"My other little friend," I say. I raise the gun in my right hand and aim it directly at Frank's chest. "Say hello to my new friend."

I see a small change in Frank's face, but he makes a valiant effort to conceal his fear. "What the hell is that?"

"It's called a gun, Frank. Want a formal introduction?"

"This is a joke. That's probably one of your brothers' toys."

I promptly shoot Frank in the leg and he falls to the ground. The sound of the gun is impressively loud, echoing through the valley. My hand is hot, vibrating from the shock. I have not fired a gun since that summer in Fenlon Falls, when I failed to take out the local wildlife with Scout's pellet gun. This is no pellet gun.

Frank's eyes have now doubled in size. They stare at me in wonderment as he writhes on the ground. I find the effect pleasing. "Jesus Christ!" he cries, gripping his bleeding leg. "What the hell are you doing?"

I step closer to him, keep the gun levelled. "I'm getting even."

"You're fucking insane, Boyle!"

"I believe that's true. I've looked into the matter extensively. At first I was in denial, but I've come to realize that that was merely one of the symptoms. After all, no one wants to admit he's insane."

"Call a doctor, you idiot. I'm bleeding." Despite the hole in his leg, Frank is still trying to be a tough guy.

"This is just the beginning, Frank. Pretty soon, your body will be so full of holes, it'll be whistling Dixie."

"Put the gun down and help me." He tries to stand.

I take several steps closer until I loom over him with the gun. "Stay down, Frank." I am all calmness.

He obeys. "This is crazy." His voice is wavering.

"How does it feel?"

"What?"

"Your leg. Does it hurt?"

"Fuck off! Of course it hurts."

"But how much? I mean, is it the worst pain you've ever experienced?" My curiosity is purely academic.

"What do you want me to do, beg for my life? Okay. You win. I'm begging. *Please* don't shoot me. *Please* help me. *Please.*"

"You don't sound very sincere."

Frank drops the sincerity, which he doesn't wear well. "You're going to go to jail for this, Boyle."

"No, I'm not."

"I'm going to press charges. I'll testify in court."

"No, you won't."

"Get me some help right now, and I promise I won't press charges."

I consider his generous offer. "Your promises mean nothing to me. You won't testify against me because you'll be dead."

He whimpers, involuntarily. "You're crazy."

"We've already covered that topic."

"You'll go to jail for life."

I shake my head. "I'm a minor. The Young Offender's Act will protect me."

"They'll make an example of you. They'll put you in a nuthouse, where you belong."

"You don't understand. I'm not going anywhere. Don't you see? I'm saving the last bullet for me."

Frank begins to cry. It is a truly pathetic sight. It disgusts me, offends me more than his cruelty ever did. "Please, no." His hands are covered with blood. But it is only a flesh wound, not life-threatening. He swipes a hair from his face and leaves a red streak across his forehead.

"You brought this down on us both, Frank. You are responsible for this."

He is really bawling, now. This is his first experience with helplessness. "I'm sorry," he mutters. He is working hard on the sincerity, but it is a new arena for him.

"You *are* sorry."

"I'm really sorry, Danny. I mean it."

"I know you do. You're sorry you are in this situation. You're sorry I'm the one with the gun."

"I'm sorry about everything."

"If I handed you this gun right now, what would you do with it?"

He doesn't answer.

"Would you shoot me?"

"No."

"You wouldn't shoot me?"

"No."

"But I shot you."

"I'm aware of that," he groans. There is more than a hint of anger in his voice.

"That's uncharacteristically generous of you, Frank."

"Give me the gun and I'll show you."

I hand over the gun. He immediately turns it on me and pulls the trigger. There is a small click, and nothing else happens.

I cluck my tongue. "That one belongs to my little brother," I say, indicating the gun in Frank's hand. I remove the Beretta from my coat pocket. "This one is the real McCoy." I prove it by shooting him in the shoulder. Another mighty boom reverberates through the ravine.

Frank screams in pain, rolls onto his back, abandons the leg for the shoulder. "Stop doing that!"

"Maybe I'll shoot your nuts off, next," I say.

He rolls onto his side, tries to get into a foetal position.

"You know, my friend Raymond said I wouldn't have the guts to pull the trigger."

"I always liked your friend," says Frank.

"I admit that I wondered, myself. I wouldn't say that I'm a pacifist, you know? I believe in the death penalty, as you may have noticed. I believe that punishment should fit the crime. I wouldn't ordinarily consider violence as my first option in any situation, but I understand that it must forever remain on the list of options." I peer down at poor bleeding Frank, with a hole in his leg and a hole in his shoulder, and an unsightly red smudge on his forehead. I still detect no remorse in his eyes. "I've run out of options with you, Frank."

"You can let me go," he whimpers. The survival instinct is strong in us all. "I won't ever bother you again." His crying escalates.

"You're weaker than I gave you credit for. I never imagined you a crybaby."

"It hurts, you bastard! Why don't you shoot yourself and find out?"

"In good time."

He mutters something.

"What?"

"I said, 'You and your fucking clichés.'"

"A good cliché is worth its salt." I have to laugh, but Frank fails to see the humour. "It's hard to see the lighter side when you're caught between a rock and a hard place."

"You're a sick fucker, Boyle."

I insert a third bullet into his other shoulder. "If you call me Boyle again, the next one goes in your head."

He mutters again.

"Stop muttering, Frank. Speak up. Have a little dignity."

"Go ahead," he says, weakly.

I shake my head. "Giving up so soon? And just when I was beginning to feel the pity welling up in me."

"See you in hell."

"Nice one," I say. "You see? Clichés can be useful in the right context." The gun fires again, this time spreading open Frank's stomach. He screams, tries to fold himself in half. "Sorry about that one, Frank. The gun went off accidentally. You'd be surprised to learn how many children are needlessly killed each year by these hair triggers. There's a lesson for everyone who keeps a loaded gun in the house."

The stomach wound is oozing a tremendous amount of blood. Frank is having trouble holding it all in. It's leaking out his mouth, too.

"You've got a little something on your chin, Frank." I point to my own chin, to help him find the spot.

He spits, stains my pant leg with his blood. Bullet number five enters his brain.

"Those were clean pants," I say angrily, to the corpse.

I stash the gun back in my coat pocket. There is one more bullet, but it will not be for me. I was leading Frank on with promises that I would be following him into the afterlife. I will let nature take its course. Suicide is for losers.

For the first time, Frank seems harmless to me. Even peaceful. I could learn to like him this way. But it is too late to foster a friendship. I have responsibilities at home that press upon me. I grab Frank by the collar and drag him toward the river's edge. As a dead weight, he is heavier than I expect. It's a struggle shifting him a few yards, but finally I have him in position.

"Any last words?" I ask the corpse. There is no answer. "Sorry. I should have asked that earlier." Without further ceremony, I roll him into the Don River. In keeping with his character, his entry is graceless. I watch him slowly drift away, toward the lake, toward oblivion. I throw the gun into the water after him and it sinks with a satisfying *plink!*

"See you in hell, old friend."

"What?" That is Raymond, emerging from the darkness—late, as usual.

"You're dripping," says Mrs. Doyle.

Danny snaps back to the kitchen. "Hm?"

"I said, you're dripping."

He looks down. There is a splatter of ketchup on his lap. "Shit." He dabs at it with his napkin.

"Language," says Mr. Doyle.

Chapter 16

"Now that you're staying in," says Peck, "can you help me with my model?"

We are upstairs, in our bedroom. The room is a mess.

"You need to spend the evening cleaning this crap up."

"I have to glue one of the wings back on," he says.

"What's the point? You're just going to leave it on the floor again, and I'm just going to step on it again. You never learn."

"I learn!" If pressed further, he will cry. Children are sensitive to criticism, especially if it's true.

I am changing my clothes. This evening's activity, I fear, will be a messy one. I select pants and a shirt from last year's fashion pile, disposable items. My ketchup-stained pants go into the hamper and my Eddie Bauer shirt gets set aside, so that my mother can sew a new button on the front. Still sulking, Peck is making a blatant effort to clean up his toys, eager to prove to me that he is capable of the chore. He is merely kicking everything under his bed when he thinks I am not looking.

"Don't just kick everything under the bed, stupid."

"I'm not."

"I'm not blind."

"I'm not!"

"I've explained it a hundred times. If you put things away properly, you can find them the next time. Remember the chess set I got you for your birthday?"

Peck does not want to be reminded of that. He lost the white bishop and two pawns before the cake was eaten. "They're not lost. I just haven't found them, yet." A child's logic is baffling.

"Clear out all the crap from under your bed and you'll probably find them."

"There's nothing under the bed."

I cross the room and get down on my knees, deaf to Peck's stubborn protests. There are so many toys under his bed, I cannot see light through to the other side. I drop the hem of the bedspread and stand up. "You probably have Jimmy Hoffa under there, somewhere."

"What?"

"Don't complain to me about not finding things until you've cleaned that mess up."

"Why are you getting dressed?" he asks, changing the subject.

"None of your business."

"Are you going out? Mom said you had to stay in."

I know his strategy. He will attempt to blackmail me into helping him with his doomed models by threatening to squeal on me. "I'm not going out."

"Can I come with you?"

"I'm not going out, I said."

"I know. Can I come with you?"

"Clean this room."

"It is clean."

Dado is tired of the conversation. At least Raymond pretends to absorb his sage advice before making the wrong decision. But common sense rolls off Peck like rainwater. Danny leaves Peck to his task, descends to the living room and settles on the sofa. He is demonstrating his capitulation to his role as babysitter. Across the room, the television rages.

Lem has control of the remote. He is addicted to *Buffy the Vampire Slayer*, which, sadly, is on one channel or another continually throughout the day. The show is ridiculous.

"Change the channel," I say.

Lem ignores me.

"I can't watch this."

Lem stares at the screen, entranced.

"How can you watch this crap?"

"Buffy's a hottie."

"A what?"

"A *hottie*."

164

"You're murdering the English language."

"It's a real word. Don't be a pompous ass." Now that Lem matches me in size and weight, he feels he can challenge my authority. But he remains a crybaby at heart.

I give him a knuckle to the arm. When the squealing subsides, I say, "Show some respect." I am secretly glad he knows the word *pompous.* He is not a total loss. If I wasn't planning to go out, I would have been forced to inflict just enough pain to wrest from him control of the evening's viewing schedule. But I don't care. I am biding time, waiting for my parents to flee the nest, so I can do the same. Lem is also biding time, waiting for my departure, so he can smoke in the laundry room, unimpeded.

At seven-thirty I call upstairs, where my parents are dressing. "Hurry up. You're going to be late." There is muttering from above. Something about minding my own business.

I wonder at times why my parents are still married. I suppose my father has looked into the matter at some point and determined that he cannot afford to divorce. Whatever it was that my mother saw in Mitch Doyle, that gleam in his eye that persuaded her to abandon her own professional aspirations, is surely gone after more than a quarter century. Six boys have cured her of any romantic fancies she might have embraced in her youth. I suspect she does not like children much. Who can blame her? After I was born, it was all downhill.

They were married for ten years before I was born. I have questioned my mother about those years, but she is not forthcoming. "We didn't do much."

"Ten years," I say. "You must have done something during that time."

"We didn't have any money. Your father was struggling to build a career. We couldn't afford to do anything."

Some things never change. We've had only one family vacation: a week at a lakefront resort in Muskoka. For six days my father sat in a darkened room, desperately trying to get a clear signal on the ancient television set so he could watch the golf match. That left my mother alone to supervise six boys, ranging in age from two to nine, as they tried to drown each other at the shore. The experience redefined for my parents what a vacation was. We've been shuttled off to camps ever since.

Raymond has been to Hawaii. Twice.

"It wasn't that great," he says. "I got knocked in the head by a surf board. I was out cold for two minutes. And I cut my foot open on the coral."

"Somehow, I can't find it in me to feel sorry for you, Ray."

"Last time, my mother got a terrible sunburn and had to spend the second week lying in bed at the hotel."

His liberal parents are taking him to Disney World as a graduation present. I had suggested that if they really cared about his happiness, they would send him there with a close friend, but they seemed cool to the idea. "You'll be eighteen, soon," I told Raymond. "You're too old to be hanging around with your parents."

"Not as long as they're paying."

No doubt my graduation present will be a new list, with revised responsibilities added to it, now that I will be an adult.

At seven-thirty-five, Dado's parents are at last standing at the front door, putting on coats and gloves.

"We'll be home by eleven-thirty," his mother says. "Don't let the boys stay up too late. It's a school night." She must repeat the obvious, ad nauseam, because that is what mothers do. "Make sure Carter does his ankle rotations."

Carter's most recent injury is a sprain suffered in a poorly explained bunk-bed incident involving Toby. Danny gives Carter marks for good sportsmanship; he has yet to officially blame Toby for anything. If nothing else, he is no rat fink.

One minute after the Doyles depart, Danny is at the door, putting on his coat and boots. There is a loud altercation taking place in the kitchen that he ignores. In the living room, another dispute is underway between Lem and Gary, who, it seems, concurs with Danny about Lem's viewing tastes. Let the monkeys settle their own scores.

Toby emerges from the kitchen altercation, victorious. I can hear Carter moaning in the background. "Where are you going?" says Toby.

"Nowhere."

"Why is your coat on?"

"You're too rough with Carter. Give the poor kid a break."

"We're just fooling around. He likes it."

"Nobody likes having his arm broken. You're turning into a bully. If you don't watch it, you'll have no friends at all."

166

"I don't need friends. I have Carter."

"Everyone needs at least one friend, kid. Think about it."

He rolls his eyes. "Are you going to the video store?" Toby knows that I don't like to bring him to the video store because he will invariably want to rent the most banal movie on the shelf, one that contains, or makes reference to, farts in every scene. I will not be forced to sit through another *Ace Ventura* sequel without a gun to my head. I have outgrown scatological humour.

"Go help Carter."

"Go stick your wang in a blender, shithead."

I make a move toward him and he flees upstairs. "I'll tell Mom you went out," he shouts from the top of the steps. A door slams and I hear Peck squeal.

If I had more time, I'd rescue Peck. I am his greatest ally in the menagerie. I am the only one who will help him repair his models, once my schedule clears. But Peck will have to fend for himself this evening. I have an appointment to keep, and I can't be late. I pull my hat down over my ears and slip out.

As I stride toward the ravine, I project myself one day into the future.

I arrive at school ten minutes early, even though Raymond is ten minutes late meeting me. We are early because, for the first time in years, we are free to take the direct route to school. We do not talk about the events of the previous night. That will be the secret that bonds us forever. The guilt of our deed is locked away—like the portrait of Dorian Gray, never to be exhumed, never to be looked upon, in all its ugliness.

As I stand at my locker and organize my books for the morning, I feel liberated, even giddy. I feel taller, as if I have grown two inches overnight. I feel *visible*. And I like the feeling.

"Hi, Danny."

I turn to face Marion Dalton. She is exquisite, in spite of the harsh fluorescent lights that give Laidlaw its institutional flavour. "Hello, Marion." I permit a genuine smile to greet her. Even the threat of Vick Peterman's fury is empty. I am no longer afraid of him. My power has been focused, centered, and I am now in full control of it. I can do anything.

When Marion moves toward me, I grip her firmly and return her kiss with unrestrained ardour. I pull her in and let her feel my new vigour. Her light cleanses me, washes away my sins, acquits me of all crimes except that of love. If I have a regret, it is only that Heidi cannot be here to witness the fruition of True Love. Had she not been shackled by the fair-game rules, it might have been she on the receiving end of my unleashed and invigorated passion. But I will not dwell on regrets. One makes choices in life, moves either toward the light or away from it. I am in the light. I am purified.

"I missed you, last night," says Marion, after we separate.

"I'm sorry, darling. Unavoidable business. *Finished* business, now, so I'll be free to go to the mall with you, after school."

She looks devastated. "I have cheerleading practice, after school." Her eyes crystallize.

"Don't be sad. We have our whole lives ahead of us." I kiss the tip of her perfect nose.

She knuckles away a tear and flips her hair. "I can't wait, Danny. I have to have you right now." Her voice wavers.

"I know where we can go. Come on."

The wrestling mats in the crawlspace beneath the stage are cool. But not for long. I look down on Marion as she writhes, moans softly, and I think of my friend Raymond. I am doomed to fulfil all his wildest dreams.

I am resigned.

"*More light and light, more dark and dark our woes!*" I say, falling away, spent.

Marion regards me as if I have suddenly grown a third arm. "What?"

"*I must be gone and live, or stay and die,*" I say.

"You're a bit strange sometimes, Danny." My words mean nothing to her, but she understands that they are good words, loving words, and she relaxes.

Exeunt.

The bell rings, verifying that they have missed roll call. The corridor explodes with bustle as the student body moves toward first period. One more lingering kiss from the lovers and they go their separate ways.

As Danny turns, he nearly collides with Heidi Borland. "Oh! Sorry. I wasn't looking."

"You were looking. You just weren't seeing," says Heidi. It is

168

evident by her expression that she has witnessed him, once again, in a clutch with Marion.

Danny sees Heidi in a new light this morning. He is tired of living in the shadows, is ready to reject the darkness. "I can see clearly, now."

"A good song, but the Shakespeare quotes suit you better, Danny."

"A good song suits my mood."

"You seem a bit rumpled. Get out of bed late?"

He shrugs, permitting Heidi to formulate her own answer, which she is naturally inclined to do, anyway. "I have to go. I don't want to be late for class."

"Saving the witty banter for Marion? You're bound to be disappointed."

"We'll see." He leaves Heidi behind, heads for the music room.

A horn blares, and I leap out of the path of the bus with inches to spare. Broadview is not a street to cross inattentively.

A biting wind penetrates my winter coat. I readjust my scarf and press on. As I pass the 7-Eleven, I spot Gutterball's lime-green Honda in the parking lot. A menacing beat pounds the landscape. The license plate vibrates noisily. Even from my position on the sidewalk, the distinct smell of pot is evident, the unlatched sunroof emitting an aromatic cloud. The tinted glass on the driver's side suddenly glides down and I see Gutterball's face behind the wheel. He is looking my way. Something silver glints in the halogen atmosphere of the parking lot. He is waving a gun under his nose. A static charge is released from within as his companions shift in their seats.

I respond to his gesture by waving a casual hand at him. I don't know if he is making me an offer or a threat. I don't care. Earlier in the day I gave him the chance to help me, and he declined. If he sits there idling much longer, he may well need the gun himself. The gangbanger factions are fiercely territorial, and Gutterball is trespassing.

The glint is gone and the nefarious tenor with the unfortunate lisp draws a line across his throat. The darkened glass rises, shuts me out. I blink and move on. I don't want to be caught in the crossfire.

Further down Broadview I pass a pair of Laidlaw geeks. I identify their faction when they are still distant silhouettes. Their awkward, bobbing gait gives them away. As we get closer, they nod respectfully and move on. I conclude by their determined speed that they are hurrying to a third geek's house, where they will waste the evening hunkered over a computer screen, playing Diablo II. I suppose, for a break, they will hack into a Pentagon computer and raise Cain with ones and zeros.

I am suddenly struck with doubt.

Perhaps Dog has been with me for so long, I don't know where I begin and he ends. I am not convinced that my judgment can be trusted, especially given the alarming blackouts I have been stricken with, recently. An hour ago it seemed my only choice was to remove Frank from my life permanently. Now I wonder. Should I not simply bear down and suffer the next few months, after which I will move on to university and leave Frank behind? Should I tell the school authorities about his bullying? Or the police? Or my parents? But I cannot tell my parents because they will not understand, will assume this torment is somehow of my own making. They will blame me for being weak. And there is every likelihood that Frank will progress to university, too. I could be stalked by him for another four years.

Until now, I have tried not to think too much about death. Murder is a sin, even for a secular soul like me. But it is hard to imagine that Frank Dolan might grow into anything more than an adult bully, a bovine thug, picking fights in dank taverns, taunting innocent neighbours, mugging tourists who wander, lost, down the wrong laneway. If only Frank were Sicilian, he might look forward to a winning career in the family business, shaking down trembling shop-owners and debt-holders. He has the brains to develop into a master criminal of Bond proportions, if such villains exist outside fiction. And whatever his potential, he must have dreams for his own future. There is even the remote hope that he will become a kind and respectable citizen. Say, a dentist; a legitimate excuse for inflicting pain.

It's too late to take up Tae Kwon Do.

No matter how thorough Dado's plan, there are variables, elements that he cannot control. The success of this event is grounded in Dado's faith in his opponent's predictable behaviour. He must cling to that faith like a zealot. But Danny is no fool. He is keenly aware that, for every crime, there are clues. He prays for few, and hopes for small ones, but there are no guarantees.

Three months from now, Danny imagines a knock at the Doyle door.

"Yes?" Mr. Doyle will use his impatient voice on the stranger. There will be no visible Watchtower, but the cheap suit will put him on guard.

"Mr. Doyle?"

"Yes. What's this about?"

"May I come in, sir?"

"What's this about?" Mr. Doyle's reluctance to let strangers cross the threshold is reflexive. Sometimes those Mormons are sneaky.

A badge will appear. "I'm Detective Morrison. Can I have a word, sir?"

They will settle awkwardly in the living room. Mr. Doyle will mute the volume on the television, but will not turn the set off. He wants to keep an eye on the leader board. He will not offer a refreshment to the detective because he is nervous. Unexpected visits from the police are always unnerving. Whatever he might have done as a hippie, he was never in trouble with the police, never had to see the authorities sitting in his parents' living room, never had to meet his father's disapproving gaze.

"Mr. Doyle, do you know a boy named Frank Dolan?"

"No."

"He was a student at your son's school."

"My son?"

The detective does not know that there are six to choose from. "Daniel."

"Right."

"He died back in February."

"You must be mistaken. He's upstairs, in his room."

"Frank Dolan."

"Oh. Right."

"Did you hear about that?"

"No."

"It appeared to be an accident."

Mr. Doyle relaxes. "What does this have to do with Danny?"

"Your son and Frank Dolan were acquainted."

"I'm sure I don't know all of Danny's friends," he admits.

"Well, sir, I gather they weren't friends."

"Oh?"

"Frank Dolan and your son had a number of altercations, over a period of time."

"Altercations?"

"My take is that Mr. Dolan was something of a bully. Some of the other children I spoke to admitted that he accosted them, at one time or another. They suggest that Mister Dolan may have been harassing your son for some time."

"How much time are we talking about?"

"Approximately six years."

This comes as a shock to Mr. Doyle. "Did you say six years?"

"Yes, sir."

"This boy was bullying my son all that time?"

"That's my take on it, yes. But I'd like to ask Daniel about it directly."

"Why would he pick on Danny? He's a good kid. He doesn't bother anybody."

"That's a question I'd ask Frank Dolan, if he were still alive. But, in my experience, sir, bullies don't need a particular reason. It's a somewhat random undertaking."

"How did this boy die? You said it was some sort of accident."

"Well, that's the thing. It seemed like an accident. That was our take on the situation, at first. But that assessment might have been premature."

"Premature?"

"It looks like it might have been deliberate."

"You mean suicide?"

"No, sir. We've pretty much ruled that out. It's looking like a murder."

"Oh."

"We believe someone murdered Mr. Dolan and made it look like an accident."

"What does this have to do with my son?"

"I'm following all leads, sir. I'm trying to talk to everyone who had contact with Mr. Dolan."

"Why didn't he tell me about this bully?"

"It's not uncommon for victims to keep silent. That's my experience, anyway."

"It's not like Danny to be silent. He's full of opinions about everything."

"I wouldn't know about that, sir. But, with your permission, I'd like to speak to him."

Danny is summoned. He has finally made time to help Peck repair his model airplanes. When he arrives in the living room, he smells vaguely of glue and paint. He shakes hands tentatively with Detective Morrison, takes his usual seat at the opposite end of the sofa from his father.

The detective begins. "You knew a boy named Frank Dolan."

Danny nods. "He was in a couple of my classes."

"You've known him for several years."

"We were in middle school together."

"His sudden death must have been a shock to you."

"We weren't that close."

"Still, when a fellow student dies it can be traumatic for some youngsters."

Danny shrugs.

Mr. Doyle cannot remain silent. "Why didn't you tell us this boy was picking on you?"

Danny shrugs again. "I dealt with it."

"How did you deal with it?" asks the detective.

"I avoided him, as best I could."

"You should have told us," says Mr. Doyle. "We could have done something about it."

"Telling you would have only made things worse."

Detective Morrison tries to take back control of the interview. "He hit you?"

"Yes."

"Verbal abuse, that sort of thing?"

"Yes."

"Did he steal from you?"

"He took my pocket money. He took one of my hats, once. I never saw him wear it. He probably threw it away. He was like that. He didn't want the stuff. He just enjoyed taking it away from me."

"Did you ever fight back?"

"Fighting back gets you nowhere with bullies. It took me a while to figure that out."

"Did he ever threaten your life?"

"Sure," says Danny. "But that's just talk. He wasn't the only one to make threats. The jocks are always threatening the geeks. That's just the way bullies talk. It doesn't amount to anything."

"Did these jocks pick on you?"

"One or two. Mostly they went for the geeks."

"Did you ever threaten them back?"

"The jocks? No. Sometimes I could insult them without their knowing it, though. They aren't candidates for Mensa."

"And what about Frank Dolan? Did you ever threaten him?"

Danny knows where these questions are leading. "Frank was smart. I couldn't insult him without getting my teeth knocked out. And I was no match for him physically. Usually, I let him wear himself out. After a while he'd get bored and leave me alone."

The detective nods. "I know it was some time ago, but do you recall what you were doing on the night Frank Dolan died?"

Mr. Doyle jumps in with his basso profundo voice. "Now, wait a minute. Are you accusing my son of something?"

"No, sir. I'm just gathering information." He turns his gaze back to Danny.

Danny is not afraid of the question. "I was here, babysitting my brothers. My parents had a function. The principal told my class about Frank's death the next morning, I remember."

"That was the first you'd heard of it?"

"Yes."

The room falls silent. Danny and the detective are sizing each other up.

"I understood his death was an accident," says Danny.

Mr. Doyle chimes in. "They think it's murder, now."

A hot flash sizzles through Danny's spine. He maintains his outward composure. "Am I a suspect, then?"

"As I've said, I'm just gathering information. We have no suspects, at the moment."

There is another lull in the conversation.

Danny swallows the panic, forces himself to remain calm. "Is there anything else you want to ask me?"

"Just one more thing. Do you spend much time in the ravine, below your school?"

"My mother forbids us from playing there."

"I see. Thank you for your time."

Two weeks later, there will be another knock at the Doyle door.

174

Imaginary Detective Morrison will not be alone. Badges will flash and handcuffs will glint. Danny's arms will twist up his back. He will, as advised, remain silent. But other Doyle mouths will work, open close open close, protesting the outrage, demanding answers. *There's been some mistake…What's the meaning…You can't take…* The words do not reach Danny. Everything is far away. He is in the tunnel with the darkness, the monumental wisp of tangible nothingness. The blackness consumes him. He is resigned.

In another universe, a single siren cries for Danny Doyle.

Masculine voices call to him through the black void. He isn't sure it is safe to answer them. They seem dangerous. His cocoon of darkness is dangerous, but it is a *known* danger. The voices are unknown. The familiar is always more comforting than the strange. There is strange comfort in the familiar danger, one enemy protecting him from another. He wraps himself in the void and bides his time.

An eon passes, and Danny awakens in a small room. When his eyes open, they are assaulted by the offensive flicker of fluorescent lighting. He is torn between the efficient use of electricity and the aesthetic damage perpetrated by such bulbs. He blinks. He is lying on a hard cot. There is a sink next to the bed, stained yellow. Someone is neglecting the housework. The tap drips monotonously. Beyond the sink is a toilet that Danny already knows he will not ever sit on any more willingly than he would sit on a pail of scorpions. He realizes that he has to urinate, and is grateful that, unlike some of the monkeys, he is able to do so while standing. The more the tap drips, the more Danny has to pee. He is beginning to wonder if he should think about where he is, but the need to urinate is overpowering. He tries to get up, and cannot. His body is not responding to his brain's commands. It's as if, after lying on the cot for two centuries, he can't remember how to move. Only his eyes and his lungs obey. He blinks a few times and begins to hyperventilate, as if to demonstrate to the rest of his body how things should go. The limbs ignore him. The hyperventilating causes him to cough, and he realizes too late that the act of coughing has released his bladder. The warmth around his hips is not comforting. On the upside, he manages to coerce his body to roll over. A good sign. The arms and legs are slower to realize that they are being called to action, but soon they are beginning to respond. A decade later, he is sitting upright, shaking, damp.

There is a flash of light, and a stranger is sitting in a chair, opposite the cot. The world is a magical place.

"Who are you?" asks Danny.

"You've wet yourself," says the stranger. His commiserating tone implies he is an ally.

He looks down at the spreading stain on his pants. "I'm sorry."

"Don't be sorry. I'll see that you get some clean clothes."

Danny regards the man in the black suit. "Are you Dog?" The man seems innocuous enough, but one can never be sure.

The man in the suit blinks at him. "I beg your pardon?"

"Are you Dog?"

"Do I look like a dog?"

Danny shakes off the notion. "Never mind. Where am I?" Now that he no longer has to urinate, the question returns.

"You don't know where you are?"

"I tend not to ask rhetorical questions."

"You're in lock-up at fifty-five division. You've been arrested."

"Oh."

"I'm a public defender," says the suit. "I've been assigned to your case. My name is James Millhouse."

Danny rubs his eyes. "I knew a Millhouse, once. He had a wiener dog named Oscar Mayer." He laughs weakly. "Isn't that hilarious?"

The suit doesn't see the humour.

"Did you ever have a wiener dog?"

"No," says the suit.

"Hm."

"You seem fascinated by dogs, Daniel."

"We never had a dog in my house, if that's what you're driving at."

"I'm not driving at anything."

"I don't like dogs much."

"Some people don't."

"We had a cat named Zippo."

"Uh huh."

"He committed suicide."

"I've never heard of such a thing."

"Oscar Mayer drowned."

"I'm sorry."

"It was my fault."

"You drowned the dog?"

176

"No. But I was responsible."

"Responsible in what way?"

"I should have prevented it from happening."

"It sounds like an accident, to me."

"Some might see it that way."

The suit shifts in his chair. "Do you often take the blame for things you haven't done?"

"Only if I'm guilty."

"I see. Is there anything else you feel guilty about?"

"Like what?"

"I don't know. How about the death of Frank Dolan?

"Frank is dead?"

"Yes. You knew that, surely."

"I'm not sure what's true, anymore. But I certainly wished is was true."

"Why?"

"To prove to me that there is justice in the world."

"Do you know why you've been arrested?"

"Something about a cottage. I put in my order, a while back."

The suit looks hard at Danny. "Before we go any further, I'm going to have a psychological assessment done. Are you agreeable to that?"

"I've looked into the matter, myself. I haven't been able to figure out what's wrong with me."

"Let me take care of it. In the meantime, I want to talk to you about your interview with the detectives."

"What interview?"

"You don't remember being interviewed by the police?"

"No."

"Do you remember being arrested?"

Danny shrugs.

"They came to your house. They brought you here. They're charging you with murder."

"It was only a dog. And I didn't mean for it to slip into the river. It was barking at a stick and lost its footing."

"It's not about the dog, Danny."

"It's always about Dog."

The suit presses on, as best he can. "Do you remember making a confession to the detectives, earlier today?"

"What?"

"You made a full confession of your involvement in Frank Dolan's death. You don't remember making that admission?"

"No."

"Hm."

"Hm?"

"You don't have to lie to me."

"I'm not lying."

"You can tell me what really happened, or not tell me. It doesn't matter either way to me. As long as you don't lie. That's all I ask. If you don't want to tell me the truth, don't tell me anything."

"Okay."

"Is there anything you want to tell me?"

"Normally, I stand up to pee."

"Of course."

The trial transpires piecemeal, coming to Danny in flashes of dialogue that do not connect. The courtroom is filled with strangers. They pace in front of him, pointing fingers, shaking heads, rattling papers. They are nothing.

A flashbulb explodes, blinding him. Men carry him. Down this, in there, through that, a corridor, an elevator, another small room. The gong sounds and he is alone.

The cottage is small, quaint, nestled beneath the trees, with western exposure to take full advantage of the sunsets. A garden hems the perimeter. A flagstone path leads to the library. There are cooking and laundry facilities in residence, so he is self-sufficient, except for the books. It is a lovely walk through the trees to the library. Once he regains his strength, he will walk the path.

There is no hurry. Plenty of time.

I must hurry. Time is running out.

Chapter 17

If Frank is punctual, I have fifteen minutes to prepare.

The temperature has dropped since I picked up Peck from McVeigh's. I pull my hat down and tug at my scarf. There is enough ambient light generated by the city that I am not working blind, but I realize too late that a flashlight would have been helpful. Regardless, I get to work.

Near the base of the steep path, the ground levels off for a few steps, before sloping downward again to the valley floor. Spanning this level spot is a row of five ancient and heavy railway ties. After a rain, these ties, with their oily surface, become particularly slick. For years I had ignored the old timber as merely part of the ravine's landscape, which is littered everywhere with detritus of bygone lives and industry. Like the crumbling quay where I finally lost track of Oscar Mayer, there is random evidence that life on an urban waterway is transient, temporary. The Don Valley is filled with history.

Early last spring I witnessed the unveiling of a mystery, as far as this wooden landing was concerned. Three municipal workmen in green coveralls and hardhats had shifted the timbers out of their place, revealing a hole, five-foot square. As they worked, I sat on the escarpment above and watched, fascinated. When one of the workmen dropped into the hole, only the top of his yellow hardhat was visible, which indicated the hole's depth. After watching for an hour, I descended to take a closer look.

"What's in the hole?" I asked one of the two workmen standing over the edge.

One of the men, leaning on the handle of a shovel, looked at me with union-bred ennui. He was an old man with skin like an over-ripe kiwi. "Routine maintenance," he said.

It was a pat answer that told me nothing. I peered down into the hole where the third man worked. There was a large steel grate that had been levered out of place and leaned against the muddy wall of the hole. The Hole Man was on his knees, bent over the opening, poking at something further down inside the drainpipe.

The revelation of this hole piqued my curiosity. I wanted more information, and instinctively knew that it wouldn't be easily pried from this low-brow trio. "I'm thinking that, after I graduate, I might apply for a job with the city. I like to work with my hands."

The second Surface Man, younger than the first, but equally as weathered and even more toothless, responded. "If you like muddy knees and the smell of shit, this is the job for you."

They all laughed.

The kiwi man said, "If you're smart, go to college. This job's for dummies." They laughed again. There was a trace of some foreign accent on the old man's tongue. Baltic, perhaps. This old geezer had no doubt fled some tyrannical homeland in search of a better life in Canada. I wondered how he felt about his new life among the free and the brave, supervising sewage.

I persisted. "I don't want to spend my entire life locked up in an office somewhere."

That did it for them. They regaled me with manly tales of their accumulated near-death experiences on the job. Collapsing retainer walls and falls from scaffolding; over-turned trucks and acetylene tank mishaps; recoiling chainsaws and badly-swung sledge hammers. The Hole Man had worked for the railroad for many years, before moving to a safer position with the city crew. He had only one lung and seven fingers remaining.

"This here spot," explained the young Surface Man, "is a Y-joint, see? Should have broke off higher. It's too low, down here. Gets plugged up every year with crud. We got to come down here and open her up, get the crud loose. That's the way it goes. Someone else fucks things up and we got to fix it."

I nodded and nodded. I didn't care about their Y-joints and crud. What caught my interest was the very existence of this hole along my familiar path. For all these years I had trod over those ties and never suspected they were covering anything. Their weight and thickness concealed the hollow perfectly. The ravine is full of wonderful secrets.

Dado stands on the landing and breathes the frigid air, takes in extra oxygen to support his muscles. He steps to one side of the timbers and squats down, grips the end of the first timber and slowly shifts it from its well-fitted slot. Because of the old tie's surprising weight, he is grateful that he never cut a single Physics class. He employs the principles of leverage and swings the beam to the far side of the landing. Four more to go and little time. He begins to worry. All he can do is work as fast as he can and hope that Frank is not early.

At last the hole is exposed. Danny is breathless, but does not have time to rest. He takes a few steps up the slope and looks down at the opening. There is enough shadow-play at the landing that one might not realize there is a hole until it is too late. He's counting on that. He descends toward the landing and spots something inside the hole. The broken handle of a shovel is resting along one side, left behind by the toothless troika that entertained him during last year's maintenance visit. He reaches for the handle. It broke close to the blade. It still has most of its length, but is ragged and splintered at one end. He knows what to do with it.

I project myself five years into the future. A ceremony is at hand. *Two* ceremonies. The first is taking place at the epicenter of exploding flashbulbs and a hysterical mob. I am emerging from the depths of a black limousine, stepping onto the red-carpeted entrance to Radio City Music Hall, in New York City. A flimsy rope barrier is all that separates me from the mob, but somehow it holds. The roar of the crowd, as they recognize me, rises and crashes like breakers on a rocky shore. I keep them at bay with a broad smile and magical wave of a hand. "Feeding the fish." That's the phrase my fiancé uses when I am faced with my swarming fans. She means it kindly.

I turn and reach for my betrothed, support her exit from the carriage. As she surfaces, another wave crashes over us. She is carefully arranged inside a silk gown that exemplifies the beauty of simplicity. Mink stoles or diamond-studded brocade or gaudy damask would only serve to diminish her natural beauty. Her strawberry hair is arrayed in an elegant sculpture that took four hours to manipulate into place. But she looks as if she threw herself together in under a half hour. A neat trick, if you can pull it off. She, too, offers nourishment to the fish, waving her free hand for the crowd. A two-carat rock glitters as the flash pots fire.

And then we are escorted across the sidewalk, through the doors to the theatre and into a vast reception room where dozens of other celebrities mingle and sip champagne. We are immediately descended upon by a clutch of important agents and producers.

"Congratulations, Danny," they say, pumping my hand, touching my shoulder.

"I haven't won, yet," I remind them. Everyone laughs at the absurdity.

"You look absolutely stunning, Laura," they croon. That may sound like typical theatrical sycophancy, but in this case it will be true.

Laura Hatley is an incontestable beauty, and a star in her own right. We were brought together for *The Crucible,* the production for which I will shortly receive my first Tony Award. The buzz surrounding my nomination for Best Performance by a Leading Actor is secondary to the vigorous anticipation of my upcoming marriage to my leading lady. Once rehearsals began, Laura and I were inseparable, locked in a bond of love that lives up to the scale of Broadway.

Marion Dalton did not take the news well. We had been together since the day after Judgment Day, the day after Frank Dolan was sent down to the brimstone mines of Hades, for blessed eternity. But once we moved to New York, Marion failed to keep up with me. Her modelling career fizzled, despite my persistent efforts to wield my growing influence in powerful circles. She was taking drugs that swung her mood wildly and did a poor job of disguising her real problem, which was her raging envy of my fame.

"It's all luck!" she rails, meaning my success. "Sheer dumb luck!"

"Hardly," I say, calmly. "Luck can get you through a door, but once you're inside, you still have to be able to pull the rabbit from the hat."

"Why do you talk like that, Danny? I don't even know what you're saying, half the time."

"Of course not, darling. You're a model."

"Fuck you! I know when I'm being insulted."

I put on my conciliatory face. "Listen, I've done everything I can to help you. But you don't show up for assignments. Or you show up whacked out on Percodan."

"It's for my back. I have constant pain, Danny. You could try a little sympathy, for a change."

182

"You're masking the symptom when you should be addressing the problem. I think I've shown tremendous understanding and patience, but only you can make your problems go away."

"Right now, *you're* my biggest problem. Maybe I should make you go away. That would be a good start."

"Now that you mention it, I've been meaning to tell you—"

I tell her about Laura Hatley. Naturally, she is the last to know. I permit her tantrum to run its course, then try to explain, but she is not receptive to my explanation, does not want to be reasonable. She has never been dumped before. She throws a bottle of Perrier at my head and thankfully misses.

"You know, Marion, it's beauty, not luck, that has opened all the doors for you. If you don't reach for those rabbit ears soon, you'll be serving french fries to pot-bellied truckers out on I-90, for two-bit tips. Pull yourself together."

I duck under a glass candy dish.

"Get lost! Go see your whore!"

Poor thing. I'll never know what becomes of her. Life moves on, and the first of two ceremonies is commencing. Pay attention:

"…And the winner for Best Performance by a Leading Actor in a Play is…*Danny Doyle.*"

The crowd goes wild. The orchestra swells. A multitude of hands reach over chair-backs to touch me, as if for luck next year. Laura kisses me. She is crying. I am crying, too. As I stride toward the podium, I forget which pocket I put my acceptance speech in. Rather than fumble for it, I choose to improvise.

Soon, I am standing in front of the microphone. A mounted medallion has been placed in my hands, and it is heavier than I anticipate. I can barely discern the audience beyond the tears and the lights, but I am aware of the red light on the television camera that lurks in the shadows. I wait for the hush and catch my breath.

"Well—" I begin. "This is a surprise." I mean my fluster, but the audience takes a different meaning from my words. A few clap and hoot. I feel my composure returning. "I can't, in all honesty, thank God and my parents for this. All three of them wanted me to study Economics."

There is laughter. Apparently I am being funny.

"Many of the people who are responsible for this are sitting out there in the darkness, or are watching this on television. You know who you are, and you know that I am thinking of you. You are all in my heart and mind."

Polite applause. My sincerity is heartfelt.

"Fame is fickle, but true talent will endure. All any of us asks for in this life is an ounce of talent, so that we might be remembered as someone just slightly more than ordinary. It's the extraordinary ones who will change the world for the better. Thank you."

Short and sweet. That's how they like it. The orchestra fires up, and I am whisked off the stage. A few official photos are snapped backstage before I am discreetly returned to my seat in the audience. Laura cannot stop crying, and who can blame her?

The post-event soiree is at Cirro's, an upscale Bistro owned by a gaggle of Hollywood movie stars who have trouble finding new ways to spend money. In the old days, they would have chartered a plane to Calcutta and delivered a suitcase of cash to a swami, for which they would have received a blessing from Ganesh and a bowl of betel nuts. Now they open restaurants or invest in Jenny Craig franchises.

The music is too loud. Conversations are shouted, misunderstood, or lost altogether in the cacophony. Laura and I evade the schmoozers by dancing. We slow-dance to every song, no matter what the beat, because we are in love. In two days' time we will be united for life in a small civil ceremony, attended by a select group of important people and the world press corps, including a crew from Entertainment Tonight.

This is only the beginning.

Dado retrieves the coil of electrical wire he stashed earlier, and ties one end around the trunk of a tree, just uphill from the uncovered maintenance hole. He throws the rest into the hole and jumps in after it. He scrapes the sewer grate with his boot, then takes the broken shovel handle and jams it into one of the spaces in the grate, twisting hard, using all his weight to secure it, until it stands upright: a single spike. He grabs hold of the wire, uses it to pull himself out of the hole, a difficult exercise with the poor footing of the soft walls. Two days earlier, it had been warm enough to rain, so the hole had begun to thaw, was now slick. By the time he is exhumed, his pant legs are damp and cold and his palms hurt. He ignores all physical discomfort. There is no time for that, now. All is nearly ready. He takes the loose end of the cable and stretches it across the path, ties it to another tree, so that it hovers about twelve inches above the ground: a trip-wire.

Danny leans against a tree and breathes deeply to calm himself. His heart pounds in his ears. He wishes he had brought water with him. His mouth is dry.

There is a sudden noise. A bolt of fear shoots through him. The sound has come from below, not above, as he expects. He has no contingency if Frank does not arrive by way of the path above. He holds his breath and prepares to run. But, except for the hum of faraway traffic, all is once again silent.

I am feeling doubt. At the final moment I wonder if I have been led astray, am making a mistake. I have always been a leader, but I sense I am the follower in this enterprise. Dog speaks to me, but he does not tell me everything. He eggs me on, but he has his own agenda. He wants me to believe he is helping me, solving my problems, but I fear he has selfish motives, and if those motives are satisfied at my expense, the more fool I. Dog lies.

But it's too late to turn back. Frank Dolan will arrive in a moment and events will unfold. A hole will be filled, if not by him then by me. Dog will have his day. He will have the last laugh, no matter the outcome.

I have made an error in judgment. I look at the hole in the ground and I want to laugh. It is a ridiculous hole. I'm in a cartoon, trapping animated lions in my ridiculous hole. Only a cartoon lion would be stupid enough to fall into my hole. I haven't even covered the hole with palm fronds, as is customary. Never mind that the nearest palm tree is thousands of miles away. And instead of an array of sharpened, poison-tipped bamboo spikes, I have a single splintered shovel handle, propped up in a sewer grate. I am as ridiculous as the hole. Perhaps I deserve to suffer whatever wrath Frank Dolan is prepared to unleash on me. Even death. If Frank is lonely, unable to foster a single friendship, at least he has never lost sight of who he is. Frank is a bully, and he knows it. He can be proud, even, of all he has accomplished in that milieu. After nearly eighteen years, I have nothing tangible to be proud of.

I project myself six months into the future. A criminal trial is concluded and I am guilty of the worst crime against society. Throughout the proceedings my name and face have been withheld from the public, to protect the innocent. Me. As a minor, I am deemed innocent, although a jury of my peers has decided otherwise. There is an obvious contradiction in that. They are protecting me, they are punishing me. I am not responsible for my actions because of my youth, yet I am a menace to myself and to the public at large.

I am a contradiction. I am a good boy. I am a murderer. Who am I? You will never know. My records will be sealed, and no doubt subsequently lost by some slack-mouthed and disaffected civil servant. I am a clean-cut kid, an honour student, a mentor, a fine example of how to not only survive adolescence, but excel at it. I am a puppet, manipulated by unseen strings, made to dance by a monumental wisp of tangible nothingness. I am a bug in a jar. I am throwing grains of sand at the elephant. Help me.

I will not spend another day in a federal corrections facility. For six months I have been waiting for my transfer to one of the lovely new prison cottages to come through. But I have just learned that the cottages are reserved for the female criminals. We don't like to punish our women because they are naturally disposed to goodness, though occasionally pushed beyond acceptable limits, more often than not by men. I have lived for half a year with eight hundred wayward boys. Most are predators. The few who are prey pay a price over and above their incarceration. I am living up to my status as a successful chameleon. I have been largely ignored by the population. Being one of the oldest boys helps gain me space. I am no longer a minor. Which is why I am being removed from the facility.

But I will not be going home. Nor will I be paroled. I am being transferred to a forensic psychiatric facility for an indefinite time. Before I am released back into the society, I must prove that I am no longer a danger to myself, or to anyone else. I have investigated the matter thoroughly, so I am confident that I will be able to demonstrate my innocence. I will make them see the strings attached to my arms and legs and mouth. I will make them see the puppeteer.

When I finally achieve my freedom, I fear I will not be welcomed home. My parents made several sullen visits before my trial began, but they explained that they were not emotionally equipped to bear attendance at my trial. I pretended to understand, but I know that I am not getting the full story. A consistent "no comment" mouthed to the press speaks loudly of their mute disapproval of me. I have failed them more completely than they could have imagined possible. My father worried that I might take drugs. He wanted to intervene, make his mark as a parent. But it never occurred to him to ask me if I harboured murderous intentions. His failure and my failure are one. The Doyles have been notified of my transfer to the psychiatric ward, but I have had no word from them. I have been hoping they would be here today, to see me off, to pay their last respects, so to speak, before the shrinks have their way with my noggin. If they wait too long, there's no telling what they will find left of their lost son. Strangely, I even miss Peck, who was a more civilized roomie than my recent companions have been.

Even more strange, I have not heard a peep from Dog since my arrest. I suppose, for him, the game is done. I am an old toy now, discarded and forgotten. He has moved on to fresher prospects.

Chapter 18

I hear footsteps above. Quiet footsteps, unmistakable. My instinct is to run, but my legs do not obey. I peer up the path and see nothing except the shadowy trees wavering. I step onto the path, below my ridiculous hole, take my place in the scene, hit my mark. I know my lines, and they were not written by William Shakespeare. Dog has supplied the script for this evening's performance, proving that not everything flows *into* a black hole.

As the footsteps approach, I apply all my concentration to making myself invisible. If I am to have any advantage at all, I need to finally pull off this feat. I know it's possible, that I am close to doing it. A strange thrill is running through me. When I dare to look down, my legs are gone. I hold out my hands, and they are not there. I want to cry out in victory, but I resist, in case my concentration falters.

I am ready for Frank Dolan.

The steps are closer now. I know from experience that it is not an easy descent. I have the patience of Job.

"Well, well," says a voice, behind me. "Look who showed up."

I spin round to face Frank. He is five paces away, below, looking warm in a thick down coat and smug in his overbearing confidence. He has snuck up from the rear after all. "You can see me?" Frank's powers are greater than I anticipated.

"I'm surprised to see you. I'd have been pretty pissed if you made me come out here for nothing. But I don't feel so bad about missing the last episode of *Survivor*, now," he goes on, calmly. "We can play our own game of survival."

"You made a mistake, coming here, Frank."

But my voice does not have his conviction, and he laughs. "I'm afraid I'm going to have to vote you off the island."

"That will be your last mistake."

He moves toward me. Once more my flight instinct ignites, and again I am unaccountably rooted to the ground. I am going nowhere. His face comes, growing immense, contorted into a lifeless mask of cruelty. My hand reaches for my coat pocket, as if controlled by an outside force. A moment later, there is a silver glint in the moonlight between me and Frank.

"Say hello to Dog," I say. My hand suddenly explodes, and Frank falls to the ground at my feet.

I look down at Frank. He does not move. I look up at the silver gun that floats, an arm's length away, at eye level. I cannot see my hand, but it feels the gun in its palm. It releases the gun and it drops to the ground, next to Frank's body.

"Danny!" calls a voice, faraway, but near.

I turn in time to see a yellow blur arc over my trip-wire, swan-dive into my ridiculous hole. A terrible ripping sound follows. Somewhere in the ether, an unseen audience applauds. I rush to the hole and look in. I see only yellow. Tears distort everything else, ripple the scene. Nothing in the hole moves.

The ensuing silence presses down on Dado, deafens him. It hurts to take in breath. If he had the strength to move, he would pick up the silver gun and put it to his own temple. Something has gone wrong.

Everything has gone as planned.

I want to die.

Everything dies.

Not you.

No. Not me.

You are death.

I am not death. But death answers to me.

I want to die.

It's not about what you want. It's never been about what you want, Boyle.

Like a ghoulish doppelgänger, Raymond appears through the trees. His yellow jacket glows. In his hand he grips the handle of a shovel, as if to taunt me, as if to deride me for not having used poison-tipped bamboo spikes. As if to say to me, "How could you do this to me, drag me into your ridiculous cartoon? You think I haven't seen that cartoon before, you idiot? Where are the fucking palm fronds?"

I cannot answer the charge. I have no defence. I notice that the shovel he holds is complete, with the metal blade intact—a manifestation also meant to mock me. The specter of Raymond will no doubt compel me to give him a proper burial with the reconstituted shovel. The least I could do for a friend.

When the ghost spots Frank Dolan, face-down on the ground, he drops the shovel and rushes to the body, turns it over. Frank's face is gone, has been transformed into a Rauschenbergian sculpture. I sense that Raymond does not appreciate the improvement.

"Pay attention, Ray. You're looking at a work of art."

Raymond looks up at me. His eyes are wide and his mouth is working, but the words float away. He looks frantic.

I attempt to soothe him. "I'm sorry about all this, Ray. Well, I'm not so sorry about Frank, but I am sorry that you were drawn into it. I never should have involved you. I knew that was a mistake, but I wasn't completely in control of myself."

Raymond stands, grips me by the shoulders, shakes me as though I were asleep.

"I'm awake, Ray. Can't you see that I'm awake?"

His voice is coming through the ether, now. "What have you done? Jesus! What have you done?" His eyes shift down to the body in the hole. "Oh, Jesus!" he cries. "Who's that?"

"I'm truly sorry, Ray."

He's not listening. He jumps into the hole. He continues to take the Lord's name in vain as he grapples with the body. "Help me. For Christ's sake, help me." After struggling to separate the body from the splintered shovel, he is cradling the lifeless form. He seems smaller, now that he is dead. "Take him," he says, hoisting the body toward the lip of the hole.

I lean down and grab what I can of the corpse. I don't see the point. We already have a perfectly good hole in which to bury him. But Raymond is insistent. I take the body from his arms and set it down on the dirty path. A small, vacant face gawps up at me.

It is not Raymond's face.

"Peck?"

He has worn his yellow scarf after all. He is a good boy.

Danny Doyle stands on the verge. Washed in pale moonlight, his silhouette briefly quivers, appears to become slightly transparent, and then disappears.